For Paul, David and Ben

CONTENTS

PART 1	THE END OF THE SUMMER	1
PART 2	THE START OF THE SUMMER	23
PART 3	THE MIDDLE OF THE SUMMER	55
PART 4	ON THE BRIDGE	153
PART 5	DARK MORNING	177
PART 6	THE TRUTH	193
PART 7	THE RAGE	205
PART 8	THE FINISH	219
	ACKNOWLEDGEMENTS	227

PART 1

THE END OF THE SUMMER

JAKE MCCORMACK

CHAPTER 1

Yesterday, I killed a boy on Clanfedden Bridge and then I drove away. Nobody had the courage to stop me. While all the other people in this town were still buzzing around at the scene of the death like little river flies, I headed straight to the town's fancy new restaurant because I wanted to leave a message there.

As I approached, the jagged remains of the restaurant's front window made weird tinkling sounds. Half-eaten meals were still on the tables. Peeled fruit and broken plates were scattered on the floor. Glasses had toppled and wine stains spread like maps of blood on the white tablecloths. All the chairs were empty. I wrote on the door:

There are times when disagreeable decisions must be made.

I stood looking for a moment at the thick curve and tilt of the letters, black and indelible. That place is mine anyway, I thought, climbing back up into my truck and heading towards Crookthorpe again. A sour stillness had seeped into the Clanfedden air. A screaming siren echoed up the hill.

As soon as things settle down again, I will drive across the bridge whenever I choose, and nobody will challenge me. They will only stare, trembling, just as they always do, at the sight of my truck with its six-foot tyres and its snarling engine. People in this town stand in awe of me when I pass. They scurry away when they see me coming, jumping into ditches or doorways to avoid me. They will not look me in the eye. Such is the nature of my power.

I am Jake McCormack.

I am the villain of this story.

I didn't start out this way. I mean, nobody's born wicked, are they? But every small town needs a bad guy, and when it happens to be you, people instantly seem to forget about any of the good things you might once have done.

I put this town on the map, kept it going, cheered us up, gave us reasons to be proud.

My shop was at the heart of this place. I never forced anyone to give me their custom. People came of their own accord.

JAKE MCCORMACK:
FOR ALL YOUR BETTING AND CREDIT NEEDS

The betting part of the business was only a bit of a laugh really: horses, football, the odds of a white Christmas, that sort of thing. There are plenty of people in this town who'd put money on two flies crawling up a wall if you gave them the chance.

But it was the credit part that really brought in the money. People needed my help, you see, and I gave it to them. I told Brian never to turn anyone away. Just as long as they were happy to agree to the terms and conditions, that was all that mattered.

I made excellent profit. Things were rolling along nicely. I'm not the one who wrecked everything. If you're looking for someone to blame, look somewhere else.

The unfortunate events of this sorry summer started with a letter.

Brian Freeman had been running the shop for me since I'd fired his predecessor, four years before. He was the one who told me about the letter in his weekly report.

'Good morning, Boss, there is some correspondence here from the leasing company. Would you like me to open it?'

I suppose I must have been busy with other matters. In the weeks that followed, he mentioned the letter a few times and between the jigs and the reels I must have forgotten to reply. Reminding me about it for the hundredth time, finally I wrote, 'Yes, all right for pity's sake, open the damn thing and tell me what they want.'

He emailed straight back: 'Serious issue, Jake. It's best that you read this yourself. See attached.' His message contained a scanned photo. I clicked it open.

NOTIFICATION

April 1st

Dear Mr McCormack

We wish to inform you that your lease at 15 Main Street, Clanfedden will expire at the end of this leasing period. The shop will be put up for auction on June 1st at 9 a.m. Before that date we ask that your fixtures and fittings please be completely removed. If, by then, they have not been removed, we reserve the right to remove them on your behalf. We have valued your business, we thank you for your custom, and we wish you every success in your future endeavours.

Yours sincerely

O'Connell Property and Leasing

I had been on the verge of a mountainous rage. But then of course, I noticed it.

'Ah for goodness, sake, I see what's going on here!' I'd clacked on the keyboard back to Brian, chuckling to myself.

'Look at the date, man! It's a bloody joke. Some idiot is trying to be funny. Take no notice. Just throw the letter away and let that be the end of it.'

But next thing, a gigantic sign went up right outside the shop, announcing that an auction was to take place, inviting people to attend. 'Someone is really pushing their luck,' I said as soon as Brian told me about this. I ordered him to get rid of the sign without delay and to keep an eye out for anything else unusual. There was a joker out there, obviously, trying to rattle my cage.

'Hello, Boss,' pinged in another message, late the next night. 'As per your recent request to keep watch, I thought you should know about this: I spotted a long-haired woman on Main Street. Definitely not from here. Very unusual-looking. Sparkly kind of coat. Loitering, you might say. Standing on the bridge, looking down at the water. Strolling around the town, peering at people, shaking their hands. Curious sort of look in her eye.'

'And?' I asked.

'Well, Jake, there's a lot of talk in the town. Nobody down here thinks the auction is an April Fool's joke at all. And that woman – I have this feeling that she and the auction may not be entirely unconnected.'

'Go to bed, Brian, and stop annoying me,' I replied, sick of the whole thing already.

'Jake, look,' his email the next morning said. 'I wonder if

this might be a good time for us to get together for a chat after all these years? I'm actually quite worried about the shop situation. I think it needs to be discussed. We must develop a strategy in case this auction business is for real. If you want to know the truth, I'm a bit concerned about my future employment.'

'Don't be an idiot,' I'd answered. 'Put all of this out of your head. You don't need to concern yourself with a strategy. Do you think Jake McCormack doesn't know what he's doing? My strategy is in place. I'll tell you about it when you need to know.'

If Brian Freeman reckoned it was odd that we'd never once met in person, he never said as much. He'd always seemed perfectly happy with the arrangement. But these recent events had flustered him. I did not like this bleating, this pestering.

Besides, I do not care to come face to face with anyone. For obvious reasons.

Brian hadn't a clue, but it was perfectly clear to me what was going on. I was sure that loser Rory Redmond was at the bottom of it. He'd tried to start some sort of movement to confront and thwart and defy me.

It wasn't my fault the people of Clanfedden all owed me money. Not my fault they couldn't back a winner to save their pathetic little lives. Not my concern they weren't able to manage their debts.

Did I pursue people? Yes, of course I did. I pursued them

for what they owed me, as any self-respecting business-person would.

No sooner had Brian Freeman taken down the auction sign, than it was erected again.

I waited till dark to drive down this time and see for myself, slowing as I passed. It loomed over my shop, right in front of the window, obscuring the door.

PUBLIC AUCTION, JUNE 1ST. 9 A.M. SHARP. TOWN HALL. SPACE LIMITED.

This was an assault on my power. This was a bid to undermine me.

Someone will regret this, I thought to myself.

I lingered on the bridge before heading back up the hill, listening to the river, fast and loud, imagining it to be the sound of blood, rushing through frightened veins.

'Should I take down the sign again, Jake?' Brian wrote, later.

'No,' I told him. 'It is time for us to put up some signs of our own. Write them yourself, in big letters.'

'What will I write?' he asked.

'Write this: ANYONE ATTEMPTING TO BID FOR JAKE MCCORMACK'S SHOP WILL BE SEEN AS A HOSTILE FORCE IN THIS TOWN AND TREATED ACCORDINGLY.

'And also write this: JAKE MCCORMACK ASSERTS

HIS RIGHT NOT TO BE UNDERMINED. BUSINESS AS USUAL.'

'OK then. I'll do that, Jake.'

There was no doubt in my mind that this would do the trick. No one would dare defy me after that. Not when I'd made my position clear in black and white. People knew better.

Nevertheless, when the end of May came, I told Jake to make sure to attend the auction, just in case. I instructed him to outbid anyone who had the foolish audacity to stake a claim on what was mine.

'How high should I go, Jake?' Brian asked.

'As high as it takes,' I replied.

This was the solution, of course, I realised, even if the auction was for real. And so after that, the disturbance that had been churning inside me settled right down. As a matter of fact, I began to laugh. I laughed until my face was sore. I laughed until my cheeks were wet. I couldn't stop.

The night before the so-called auction, I was late going to bed, but I slept deeply, and woke feeling refreshed, and got on with my usual routine, glad that this was the day the silly business would be resolved, and everything could go back to normal.

Sometime into mid-morning, sipping a cup of tea, I checked my email.

From: Brian Freeman

To: Jake McCormack

Subject: NOT GOOD NEWS

It's gone, Jake. Your place has been sold to another bidder. I've been trying to call.

I hated talking to Brian, or to anyone, but this was an emergency.

'I thought I told you to outbid anyone who showed up!' I shouted down the phone.

'I did, Jake. I did. Or should I say I tried. They said it was not permitted.'

'What do you mean?'

'They told me I was ineligible on account of being a representative of the previous tenant. It's got to do with the nature of the business. The thing is, Jake, they don't want a betting and credit shop on Clanfedden Main Street. Not any more. That's what the auctioneer said. It all happened so fast.'

I could hear Brian's nervous breath on the other end. I let the silence stretch out. He was right to be nervous.

'Who's the buyer?' I asked at last.

'The woman. That woman I was telling you about with the glittery coat.'

'I don't give a crap about any stupid coat. I want her name. Tell me her name, Brian.'

'OK, right, yes, of course. I've written it down. I have it

somewhere here. Hold on till I check.' Brian Freeman stuttered and coughed. Then there was silence, and then the rustle of quivering notebook.

'Spinelli,' he said eventually. 'Ariana Spinelli.'

Somewhere, deep inside my brain, I felt a rusty cog begin to twitch and whirr.

I hung up while Brian was still twittering on the other end about his income and his livelihood and his future. I walked to my hall door and I opened it, staring out into the grey middle distance.

Ariana Spinelli. She was back. Back at last.

Crookthorpe Hill sits high and forested up above Clanfedden. It is a maze of lanes and trees, a patchwork of fields. From the front door of Crookthorpe House I can usually see the dim lights of the town below, twinkling faintly up from the valley. But that evening, an unusual fog had settled and I could see no lights. It had grown cold and suddenly windy, and a hard rain was falling. A vague, blurred moon had appeared. Smears of cloudy darkness stretched across the sky. I stood there, staring out, imagining the raindrops to be frenzied tadpoles; imagining that inside the wind there was a human voice saying something I could not hear. Anger spat and sputtered inside me like bacon on a griddle. A violent wetness soaked my skin.

CHAPTER 2

Brian Freeman must have been the only person in Clanfedden who'd never known Ariana Spinelli. 'Before my time, boss,' he'd said. Ariana Spinelli. Rachel Reilly. They'd once been the saints of Clanfedden.

Ariana and Rachel. A pair of constant stars, people said. I'd spent years trying not to think about all their so-called beauty and goodness.

Funny how neither of them could be relied on in the end. After one of them was dead and one of them was gone, people often said that Clanfedden had lost its sparkling compasses.

Ariana never came back for Rachel's funeral, which tells its own truth about how much she actually cared about her, or any of us.

It had been twenty years since Ariana last walked the streets of this town. It was too late, I hoped. Too late for her to expect any kind of welcome. There was some lukewarm comfort in this thought.

The comfort didn't last long. The following weeks were filled with a whole miscellany of unpleasant surprises, and everything moved very fast.

Brian was weak, of course, cowering in the face of officialdom as weak men always do. He let them all in. A team of builders in *my* shop. All women. Have you ever heard the like? And he stood by and watched as my counters, my lino, my posters, my tills, my stools, my noticeboards, my Perspex booths were torn from their fixtures. All ripped and bent and broken, thrown out on to the road.

I made many phone calls of course, went through all the official channels, letting them know I had no intention of taking this lying down.

In infuriating monotone, Craig Kenny, the property company man repeated that I, Jake McCormack was ineligible to bid on account of the nature of my business.

Right then, next step. I appealed to Kenny's boss, Quinn.

'The town council has decided,' Quinn explained. 'This sort of enterprise has been no good for Clanfedden. It's time for a change.'

Ah, the town council. I knew for sure then that Rory Redmond was behind this, just as I'd suspected.

I clenched my jaw till one of my teeth cracked.

Damn you, Rory Redmond.

A plague on you, Ariana Spinelli.

*

Jake McCormack isn't accustomed to being shafted. This was not the natural order of things and everyone must have known it. Not even a conversation with the top man, O'Connell himself, made any difference. You'll regret it, I told him, after which he terminated our call very swiftly.

I drove into town again after that, this time to see if I could get a look at her. Evening sunshine sliced the air as I turned the corner into Main Street. I did not like to appear in daylight, but I felt compelled to see her for myself. I parked a way back, kept my balaclava on. I waited with the engine still running, noticing a strange, stripy car, like something a clown might own. After a minute or two, a shadow darkened the doorway of the shop. Someone was inside there already, I realised, grinding my teeth again, gripping the steering wheel, keeping very still.

And then she stepped out into the light.

Her hair was grey now, but wild as ever, and Ariana Spinelli still sparkled.

She put her hands on her hips, seeming to take a very deep breath, and she looked up and down Main Street. She opened the boot of the ridiculous car, pulling out a huge box, hauling it towards the shop.

Many of the people of Clanfedden were coming out of their houses and they were looking at her too, their heads held in various angles of friendly delight.

Idiots, all of them. Easily dazzled.

Not me, though. I knew her game.

That place was mine. People should have respected that. *She* should have respected that. But Ariana Spinelli had never respected me.

She paused in the act of lifting another box, glancing in my direction now. And though obviously she could not see my face, I didn't hang around. I'd only wanted a glimpse of her anyway. I revved up and screeched past.

I suppose it was inevitable that inane town babble was to follow. Brian was full of it – how the whole place was in a state of high excitement. How they were all talking about the glamorous, the interesting, the talented Ariana Spinelli, back in their midst. There was stupid chatter from those who did remember her. How wonderful it was. How she seemed to glitter. How cheering it was to be reminded again of her loveliness and her unusualness: those enormous rings she still wore on her fingers; those earrings that tinkled like little bells whenever she was near! How full of freedom and optimism she was! How happy they all were to see she'd come back, just like she'd always promised.

It made me sick to hear of it. But I am not an unreasonable person. Perhaps she hadn't actually seen the signs. Perhaps she didn't understand that it was *my* property she had stolen. Perhaps there was a chance she'd made an innocent mistake. After some reflection, I decided I would give her an opportunity to change her mind.

I reassured Brian that he still had a job, but that for the moment, he'd have to work from home. I told him I needed him to keep me informed of the developments. A lot of things were happening that needed to be monitored, and they were happening at the speed of sound.

Within a few days, I'd sent him to put things to Ariana Spinelli in clear and certain terms. 'Tell her she'll have no luck in a place that really belongs to Jake McCormack. Explain that any business she starts there will die before it gets off the ground. Make her understand who she's messing with.'

'OK, Jake, I'll do my best,' quaked Brian down the phone.

'Boss,' he reported back a day later. 'She said you were perfectly entitled to express your views, but she was busy. She wanted me to tell you that you're welcome to come yourself and discuss the issues that are troubling you. She said she understood why you would find these developments disagreeable but there are times, she said, when disagreeable decisions must be made.'

I wouldn't forget those words. She'd be sorry she spoke them. In time those words would echo back to her. For that was the moment when any chance of Jake McCormack's mercy disappeared. Ariana had come here specifically to profit from the opportunity of my loss.

She had always fancied herself full of magic dust. She wanted to sprinkle it everywhere. As if anyone had asked her to.

It doesn't work like that, Ariana. You can't float back into this town you abandoned and make yourself at home. You're not a gift sent from heaven, whatever you might think.

A lot has happened since you left. Welcome to the new Clanfedden. You shouldn't be hopeful and bright and full of purpose. You should be afraid.

I suppose I should have remembered that Ariana Spinelli wasn't afraid of anything. It was her fearlessness that made her so full of hope and purpose at the beginning of the summer. But courage is not always a virtue.

She had brought a boy. Her son. An accomplice in her mission to douse us all with glory and light.

He was a helpful boy. He worked diligently in that restaurant. Within a week of arriving, he'd gone with his mother to put flowers on Rachel's grave, a gesture that instantly warmed all the needy little hearts of Clanfedden.

I alone knew that she and her boy spelled catastrophe.

An angel, just like his mother, said the people of the town, not realising that beauty like this is a dangerous thing.

I wonder what they'd have said if they knew back then that this day was coming? If they knew that soon her beautiful son would be dead?

They'll get used to what has happened. Like young children, foolish small town people always adapt. From now on, Clanfedden's story is simply going to have a new cautionary chapter in its history and a new image, hazily drawn, of Luca Spinelli standing in front of me on the bridge, telling me that I cannot pass.

How could anyone have thought there would be no penalties? How could anyone have failed to understand that Jake McCormack does not back down?

Dawn is breaking now and I can see the line of Crookthorpe's horizon, harsh and clear. There are still some ends to be tied up. Allie Redmond is injured and while she has tried to get away from me, she is sure to be somewhere nearby. She won't have got off this hill, not in her condition. I'll be heading out again in a minute to deal with the situation.

I didn't think anyone would have the nerve, but after the events on the bridge last night, Allie Redmond must have tailed me, and she must have gone to the trouble of reading the message I left on Ariana's door, and when she made it up Crookthorpe Hill after me and started hammering on my door, this is what she screamed:

'It was not a disagreeable decision! It was murder!'

And then she went on about how Luca Spinelli was her best friend and how I was a monster and 'what have you done' and other dramatic stuff like that.

There's no one more wide awake than a fourteen-year-old, I suppose. At that age, they're not capable of weighing things up properly. Some call it the courage of the young but it's really the ignorance of inexperience – a foolish sense of righteousness – a complete lack of insight about the consequences of certain actions. Holy hell, it's a miracle that any of them survives.

Fair dues to her, though. Allie Redmond. How she must have steeled herself to try to face me down. What resolve, what grit it must have taken for her to do the things she did. How fiercely she tried to stand up for her little friend, even though it was too late.

She didn't have the right to trespass. A person's house is their dominion. I couldn't let word get around that a *girl* had gained entry at the gates of my home. She had to learn. Another line was going to have to be drawn.

I was ready for her though, for it is in my nature to be

ready for anything. I stood in the hallway checking my balaclava and I opened the door.

'Stay exactly where you are,' is what I said, using the voice that has haunted many a Clanfedden nightmare. 'Come no closer.'

'I'm not afraid of you any more!' she replied, though it was obvious she was terrified. Still, she lunged across my threshold and grabbed on to me and pulled at my balaclava, ripping its dark wool off my face and we both stood there then, shocked and silenced by what she had just done.

'Oh God,' she whispered, and a huge shudder seemed to overtake her, the reality of my face being even more horrifying, obviously, than all of her imaginings.

She turned and ran from me but she had not seen that the gates had closed behind her. She had not known there was no easy way out. Like a frightened animal she climbed my pointed fence.

I couldn't leave her there writhing with her leg caught on that spike. The noise of her fading groans was a distasteful sound. In my own good time, I fetched the ladder. I climbed up and lifted her off and dropped her down on to the other side, where she lay, grunting softly.

I hurried in to the house again to get my coat and the necessary equipment. Look where her foolishness had got her. I'd prefer to have avoided this, but now she too could not be allowed to live. I'd have to hide her well, afterwards.

I can only have been gone back into the house for a minute or so. When I came out again, the brat was gone. Never mind, I thought. The little cockroach won't have got far.

But last night the darkness was a deep and solid thing, and by then the rain had started, and if her blood had made a trail, I could not see it.

Images of yesterday's happenings come back to me in random order now: the empty space on the ground where Allie Redmond should have been; her leg impaled on my fence, a strange sound of disbelieving pain coming from her, each breath a little explosion; Ariana, running towards the bridge, shouting like she'd gone insane; Allie standing in my doorway, my woollen mask in her trembling hand; Luca, standing opposite me on the bridge, his short life coming to its defiant end; the empty restaurant; the smashed window; the spilt wine; and everything broken in this town, and its people stunned and frozen, and all the lights gone out.

PART 2

THE START OF THE SUMMER

LUCA SPINELLI

CHAPTER 3

No one from Ashfield Secondary was allowed to talk about what had happened on the third-year school trip to Paris.

'Let it just be said,' Mr Kilkenny announced during a special assembly, 'that there was an unpleasant incident. And any talk or reference to it must cease immediately. There is to be no idle chatter and no speculation and no gossiping. It has certainly not been edifying for anyone involved. The less said about it from now on, the better.'

Tom Cranfield was sitting beside me, as if that was going to make any difference. For a microsecond, his arm accidentally touched mine, but I moved my chair away. Obviously, we did not speak.

People turned and stared at us when Mr Kilkenny was speaking because everyone knew who'd been involved. We weren't the only ones, but we were the ones who came out of it the worst, for reasons I don't want to go into, and probably never will.

Mr Kilkenny said lots of things that morning, like:

'You should all be able to think more clearly, now that the heat of the incident has passed.'

And:

'It seems that some sort of fleeting madness overtook students on the trip.'

And:

'Everyone should be able to move on without being for ever defined by such a short moment in time.'

I tried, I really did. But the memory of it wouldn't leave me alone. Like a heavy stone inside me, it weighed me down, and made even the simplest of ordinary tasks feel more or less impossible. The others were able to carry on normally, but I found that no matter what I did to erase the thing from my head, I just could not forget.

In the weeks that followed, the atmosphere at home was tense and unusual. My mother stared for hours into our laptop (a thing she was always saying no one should do), her face washed in white-blue digital light, a frown puckering her forehead, her voice muttering.

She tried to repeat the same kind of things my teachers had said. 'You are a good person, Luca,' she said, and, 'nobody should be defined by a single moment in their lives.'

'Yeah, yeah. I know,' I replied, even though I did not know, and, 'Thanks,' I said, even though I wasn't grateful.

The incident had twisted something inside me. It was as if some big, important tunnel to my heart had been crushed and squashed and damaged and could not be repaired. There had never been so much silence between us.

I couldn't really be bothered to ask but I knew my mother was up to something. For the whole of May she kept going out into the garden to talk on the phone. When she came indoors again her hair would always be covered in pink petals from the cherry trees, which made her look sort of crazy. In the evenings once dinner was over, she would take out the big clackety calculator on which she carried out feverish computations, scribbling big numbers into her notebook.

Then very early on the first day of June when it was not yet light, I woke to see my mother standing in the doorway of my bedroom like she was a ghost.

'Luca. Luuuuca.'

'What?' I said.

'I am going on an important errand; I won't be home till very late. There is basil and tomato soup on the stove, and fresh bread in the oven that needs to be taken out at nine a.m. on the dot. I've left cannoli in the fridge. You must bring them to room temperature before you eat them.'

Before I had a chance to switch my lamp on, she was gone from the doorway. I crawled out of bed and watched her from the window as she pumped up the tyres and checked the oil and threw her big leather bag in through the window of the passenger side.

It was midnight when she returned.

'*Amore mio*,' she said, sitting on the end of my bed, 'are you asleep?'

'I was,' I answered.

'Come,' she said, handing me my dressing gown, 'come down to the kitchen for some gingermint tea. I have news!'

I didn't really want to, but if you knew my mother, you'd know how hard it is to say no to her.

So I sat as she boiled the kettle and waited until the tea was exactly the right golden colour. She coughed, the way people sometimes do before making a great announcement. I forced a sip or two, still groggy, still confused.

'A little while ago, I made a decision,' she said then. 'And that decision has taken me on a journey and today I have made that decision come true!'

'Mum, it's the middle of the night. Can you please stop talking in riddles? Could you just cut to the chase?'

'I have purchased a premises!'

'What? Where?'

'It's a shop, which will soon be our restaurant! With living quarters upstairs! It is far away from here! There is no time to waste. Once a decision like this is made, the only thing is to get on with it as quickly as possible. *Colui che esita è perduto.* How do you say that in English?'

'He who hesitates is lost?'

'Yes, exactly, good boy, I knew you'd understand. I am sending the builders tomorrow to start the work. And next week you and I embark on this adventure together. New beginning. Fresh start. Everything will be excellent. Everything will be fine.'

A cold jolt of wakefulness hit me like a slap.

'Hang on a moment. How will everything be fine?'

'Because, *mi amore,*' she said, beaming, 'we're going to the one place I should have taken you to a long time ago, and, oh *allora*! It is so clear to me now!'

'Where?'

'Clanfedden! How could you not guess? The time has come at last.'

'Wow. Really?' I said, rubbing my eyes.

Clanfedden. I mouthed the name to myself, as recognisable as a taste.

'Yes!' she said. 'How foolish I have been, staying away for all these years! How important it has been for me to change my mind!'

For a town I'd never been to in my life, I knew a lot about Clanfedden. It was the magical village of my mother's memory, the glimmering place that she'd told me about so many times. When I was a kid, before I went to sleep, she'd pull the covers over me and snuggle me in, knitting her stories of Clanfedden into the pattern of my own childhood dreams.

When she'd been young, long before I was born, my mother had spent *seven sparkling summers* there. She'd had a best friend called Rachel. Together they had many adventures during those *sunny seasons of great happiness.*

Her stories had fixed coloured pictures in my head, of a pretty town all nestled in a green velvet valley with forest hills above, of tennis courts and a splendid playground and a small but perfect library that was also a post office, halfway up a hill. Of a girl called Rachel and a boy called Rory and a main street where each house was painted a different colour like a box of crayons.

Clanfedden was where we were supposed to go when we first came to Ireland, but in the end we never did. All it had taken was for my mother to speak the word to make it feel like an old, long-forgotten secret was coming back to life.

'What happened, Mum?' I asked, wondering why I'd never asked before. 'Why did we never go in the first place?'

My mother's eyebrows rose into astonished arches. 'Because of Rachel, of course,' she said. 'I'd been too sad.

'I wrote to her for years after my last summer there. I didn't know then that I'd never see her again. I sent her a card and a picture when you were born but she never answered that either. It was different in those days. Harder to stay in touch. But I never forgot. I was determined that we would connect somehow. I had planned to surprise her as soon as we got to Ireland. I was going to arrive with no warning. I couldn't wait for her to meet you. I couldn't wait to see her again myself. And then, well, when I found out she had died . . .'

For a second, my mother stared off, as if looking at some strange and distant thing. And then she shook her head and waved her hands like she was swatting away an insect.

She sniffed and patted down her hair and grabbed the sweeping brush, stroking it across our already-clean floor.

'But now . . . you see. Through timing and through research, I have happened to learn of this wonderful business opportunity right in the centre of the very same town. Luca, I have grabbed it with both hands. There is magic still there, I feel sure of it. I have been afraid – afraid of tarnishing my gilt-edged memories. But no longer! I've seen it with my own eyes! Parts of it are greatly changed, but the heart of the place still beats, and it is beckoning me just like an old friend might. It is the perfect solution for us both. It is fate. It is destiny.'

My mother's enthusiasm was usually unshakeable and infectious, but at the time it had not been easy for me to feel confident or excited or hopeful about anything. Even after everything that had happened, leaving town felt like a radical step. And even though Clanfedden always sounded like a magic place, I think she saw the doubt in me.

'Look, if it doesn't work out, we don't have to stay there. Every decision is reversible. What's the harm in giving something a try?'

'Let me think about it for a while, Mum,' I said, before going back to bed.

It wasn't too long before I could feel the warmth of her sunny mood. Old anticipation began to wake up in me. Maybe getting away from here and going there *would* help make things better. Maybe Clanfedden *was* the answer.

Our neighbours threw a goodbye party.

'How can it have come to this?' wailed Caroline Fahy from two doors down.

'Who will make pistachio cannoli for us now?' said Peter O'Farrell, gazing at my mother, his eyes full of actual tears.

'Oh, nonsense,' tutted my mother gently. 'They are as easy as pie! I shall write the recipe out before I go.'

'We're going to miss you so terribly,' insisted Sally Brady, grabbing my head and pressing it against her enormous chest.

'I know,' I said, doing my best to struggle away.

And all the time, beneath the clink and murmur of the party, there was talk about how senseless it was for us to be leaving.

'We thought this was your home. We thought you loved it here!' they said

'I have unfinished things to attend to in Clanfedden, and I have made my decision,' my mother explained each time, and that was basically that.

It wasn't until later, when the crowd had thinned, that Frank Cranfield, Tom's dad, showed up. He walked right over to me. I felt a gulp in my throat. He held out his hand and I shook it, but I could not look into his eyes or even at his face.

'Listen, Ariana,' I heard him say later. 'I hope you don't mind me asking. It's not because of the . . .the incident on the school trip, is it? Because if it is . . . well, honestly these things blow over. People forget, especially at that age. In time it won't seem so bad. Surely there's no need to be taking such dramatic measures.'

My mother's shoulders seemed to rise as she faced him.

'Frank, please do not attempt to diminish what has happened. What our boys have been involved in,' she replied, and her words came out quick and sharp, little splinters of ice.

Noticing me on the stairs, they both lowered their voices then so I could not hear the rest.

*

'Everyone knows, don't they?' I said later when the party was over, and I was helping her pick up the rubbish and collect the glasses.

'Oh Luca, love. Please, you must stop tormenting yourself.'

There were other conversations too, ones that my mother used her hushed voice for. A chat with Mrs Delaney across the road and a deathly quiet phone call with her friend, Petrova. Everyone knew the truth, of course they did. It's just that none of them would talk about it.

Strictly speaking it was none of my business but I kind of wished my mother would cut her enormous hair. She said I used to love putting my fingers through it when I was little, when my 'knuckles were dimples', but these days I thought her hair made her look a bit mad. She wore a ton of jewellery all different colours – very big rings on her fingers and earrings that sounded like wind chimes, and she often went around the place in a shining kind of coat covered in sequins and little coloured beads, something that nobody else would ever wear.

There were other things that made her seem different too. Our *Cinquecento* was very old and its engine sounded like a hairdryer, not a car, and it was painted with three broad stripes. Green, white and red.

'For Italy!' she proclaimed loudly whenever anyone asked about it, which they often did.

When I was small, instead of bedtime stories my mother often read me recipes from the Spinelli Family Recipe Book, an ancient cookbook that had been in our family for many generations. I was not a kid any more, but sometimes she still read to me from it, her voice dramatic and passionate as she recited the ingredients and instructions for family favourites like *spaghetti alla vongole* or garlic soup or *melanzane alla parmigiana*.

The Friday before we'd left for Clanfedden, she had taken down the book to read.

'Mum, really, come on, there's no need. Not any more,' I tried to explain. 'I know them off by heart.'

Her eyes went glossy then and I thought she might cry, a thing I'd rarely seen her do, but always dreaded.

'Oh, Luca!' she sighed. 'You don't want to hear them any more?'

'Not really,' I answered, wishing I'd said nothing. 'I mean, you've read them a million times.'

'Do you tell the sun not to bother rising, because it rose yesterday? Do you tell the seasons not to come around again? Or the plants not to flower, just because they have flowered before?'

'No, I don't. But that's not the same thing.'

'Of course it is. *E lo stesso.* The same. These are our stories, *mi amore.*'

There was a sad, slow tick-tock then – the nail of my mother's index finger tapping on the hard, dark cover of that old book.

I used to think she was magic.

To my mother, food and the kitchen were the things of paradise. When she was cooking, it was as if a thousand dazzling notes seemed to play. Sharp, zesty lemon; rich, sweet tomatoes; strong, peppery basil would mingle in the air with the sounds of her soft singing. Misty baby-memories would come to me when she cooked: a white rocky cove, the pale stone of an outdoor oven, a blank blue sky, a gleaming turquoise sea.

'To make a meal is to embark on an adventure,' she often told me, which sounded comforting when I used to be a kid and when I still believed everything she said.

I didn't say goodbye to anyone at school. I stopped checking my texts because there were like a hundred from Tom Cranfield, none of which I was ever going to answer or even look at or read.

No one else from my school phoned or called to the door or texted.

We stuffed the car with boxes full of our most important belongings. The neighbours came out to say more farewells, pressing gifts into our bags.

There was barely any room for me in the back of the

car, but somehow I managed to squash myself in, smiling at the neighbours even though I didn't really feel like it. My mother started the engine, rolled down the window and waved her big-jewelled hand to the crowd. 'Here we go!' she said, turning up the music as we moved off.

I slept on the journey, dreaming of the school trip to Paris, and in my dream, I fixed the things that had been done wrong, and everything was different and everything happened in the way I would have liked it to. I dreamed too of our wonderful new destination – its flowers and tennis courts and playground, its river, its valley, its library-post-office.

I don't know how long I slept for but I woke to a bumpier road, keeping my eyes closed listening to the screeches and judders of the car. There was a sudden chill in the air. The music from the radio faded in a splutter of white noise and then disappeared into silence.

'Luca!' my mother said. 'Wake up! Look! It's Clanfedden. We are here!'

Which is when I opened my eyes to a new and awful world.

CHAPTER 4

The town sign hung rustily off its hinges and there was a terrible smell in the air. We drove past boarded-up buildings, empty shops, a grim, grey school. I stared out, my body tense with dismay, my heart empty.

A broken playground came into view. There was a slide, cracked and buckled, and staring plastic horses on a lopsided carousel. Big, crumbly, corroded nails poked from a crooked climbing frame. Two single swings swayed in the air. DANGER KEEP OUT said another scruffy sign.

Three men in hoodies stood by a warped seesaw, huddled together, the little orange ball tips of cigarettes swelling and shrinking in the thickening dark.

'I couldn't believe how affordable the property prices were,' chirped my mother. 'An incredible opportunity. Of course it is a pity that parts of the town are so run down now.'

'*Run down*?' I said, a well of horror throbbing in my stomach. 'And what do you mean "a pity"? Mum, this place is a disaster. It's nothing like you described. Look around. Even the playground's like a crime scene.'

'It's somewhat changed, yes, indeed it is. I mean, it has been twenty years,' my mother replied, her shoulders set, her gaze strong. 'Come, Luca, let's not make snap judgements. There is so much to explore.' She parked on the main street, leaping out, forcing me to get out too. She stood, hands on her hips, looking up and down.

I walked behind her, staring into the shops in silent shock, at cobwebs under warped old shelves; at hairy white spider nests wedged in forgotten corners; at dust twinkling in the last of the light.

Up ahead was a shopfront even worse than the rest, with a huge pile of rubbish outside.

'This is it,' she breathed, stopping in front of it. 'I am so glad we came. We can rescue this building, turn it into something beautiful. This is the time, Luca, and here is the place, and we are the people.'

That was the moment when I began to feel properly afraid.

'Mum, how could you?' I whispered.

'I know it looks a little – how do you say—'

Often when excited and sometimes when stressed my mother would forget how to speak English, and I'd have to help her.

'Creepy? Horrible? Crap?' I suggested.

'No, no. I mean yes, it needs us to . . . to . . . *agghindare*, maybe,' she said.

'Bloody hell, Mum, it needs a lot more than that,' I replied, since *agghindare* means simply to primp something up, something that's already fine.

'There has been damage and decay in this town, that is certainly true; but we must give this place a chance. Stop jumping to conclusions.'

We stepped inside. It was all empty and wrecked.

'In need of work, admittedly, but the proportion is perfect. Just the right amount of space,' declared my mother. She strode to the back of the room and tried the handle of another door, which creaked open. Stale gusts of musty air rose. The walls were damp to the touch. I froze at the sound of footsteps coming from above but it was only the builders.

'Hello, hellooo, is that Ariana?' Three women in overalls stomped down the stairs shaking hands, one after the other, with my mother. 'We are making good progress,' said one. 'But don't come up yet, we need a little more time,' said another. 'Yes, we are making it safe,' said the third, whatever that meant.

'Perfect, let's have a stroll around town while we're waiting,' my mother suggested, and without having an alternative, I followed her.

'Things will change. Things will happen.'

'What does *that* mean? What things?' I asked.

'Things that will make you feel different,' she said.

Nothing was making me feel different, and nothing was going to. Everywhere I looked, there was something that made me want to cry. A dirty fence, a padlocked door. Right behind the shop, down a cracked pavement there was a rubbish pit with a rusted fence around, wrecked and stinking, full of black shiny bags oozing horrible dark juices.

'The tennis courts! Oh my goodness, the hours we spent!'

I wasn't sure if my mother was even talking to me. I thought about how different her descriptions had been all these years, compared to the scenes in front of us. I remembered the dreams I had about Clanfedden. I remember falling asleep to the imagined *pock-pocks* of tennis ball and racket mingling with the sounds of friendly laughter.

'How lovely it still is!' she whispered when we reached Clanfedden Bridge where nearby trees were bent and warped and brittle and where floppy flowers in their baskets dangled ragged above the dark water. 'Listen to the sound of the flowing river! Look at the magnificent flash of the bridge's granite!'

'Mum, Seriously?' was all I managed to say, because if there was a prize for the saddest, most depressing object on the planet, Clanfedden Bridge would have had a strong chance of winning.

When the builders phoned my mum to say we could go upstairs, we returned to the shop.

'Wait till you see what they'll have done!' said my mother. As if upstairs was going to be any better.

We climbed the staircase.

I leaned against the wall when we got to the top, as if otherwise I might fall, trying to stay calm. Slowly I counted fourteen dead flies on the faded carpet. It was going to be an awful place to live.

The next morning a hard, curtain-less light plunged through the window. Remembering where I was, in this tiny bedroom above the world's dustiest, emptiest shop, I winced.

Beep-beep-beep sounds floated up from the street. I could hear my mother's voice chatting away, all jolly and thrilled as if nothing was wrong and as if no one's life had basically been ruined.

I staggered downstairs. It felt like there was fog everywhere. Removal men were unloading the boxes and the builder women were giving directions. My mother was there in the middle of it all, a blaze of business and delight.

In times of despair, being surrounded by other people's cheerfulness only makes things feel worse – the way Christmas might feel when you're poor, or birthdays must feel when you're old, or Valentine's Day feels when no one even likes you.

My mother made sure to keep her gingermint tea in her handbag so she could make it at a moment's notice without having to unpack, 'for anyone who needs a pick-me-up'. She claimed that it cured every ill. 'It's important for people to take breaks!' she shouted to the removal people and the builders who all seemed to know each other. Over tea she asked each of them where they were from and about their families. One of them showed her a photo on a phone and she gasped, claiming she hadn't seen such a beautiful baby since her own baby had been born, pointing then at me. And all the workers nodded their heads and grinned, and my legs felt weak and there was a pain in my heart.

I walked outside to see if air would make me feel better. Someone had put our orange sofa down on the street in front. I sat on it, feeling dazed.

'Nice to see you beginning to feel at home, Luca. But maybe wait until the furniture is inside, hah?' my mother shouted at me, her tea break over, hauling two bags along the ground towards the door. I stood to help, crouching to lift one of the boxes.

'That's fragile, *mi amore*. Leave it please. Read the labels!'

Each box had a giant white sticker on it with a single word in my mother's curly capitals. FRONT KITCHEN. BACK KITCHEN. STORE ROOM. OFFICE. LUCA. MISC. BREAKABLE.

I grabbed another box.

'Not that one, Luca. *C'è un sistema*. There is a system.'

I tried to move the sofa.

'Stop, Luca, no!' she said, and the three builders butted in too, telling me I'd only wreck my back if I did it the way I was doing it.

'Look,' I said in the end, 'maybe I should just go for a walk.'

'*Bene! Un'esplorazione!* That's the spirit! Here, let me draw you a map to the library-post-office. I knew a girl who worked there once.'

'Yeah, all right,' I said dully. At least I'd be able to get some internet there.

I passed the huge broken sign again.

W LCOM TO CL N EDDEN.

Sharp dots of rain began to land on the top of my skull as if somebody was aiming them at me.

I walked and walked, trying not to look at the scraggly fields and the grey brick and the crumbling paths. Maybe there was no library any more. I wouldn't have been surprised, considering how everything I'd been told about this place was a lie. I peered at my mother's map. It was just a load of scribbles and illegible shapes.

People stood in the doorways of small houses, staring as I walked by.

I stopped in front of one of them, where there was a tiny smiling old lady with hands like the bark of a tree. 'Hello,' I asked her, feeling awkward. 'Is . . . is there still a library here?'

And then suddenly there was a whole crowd of people bunching around me, engaged in an instant competition of shouted directions. My low-level panic sharpened, but I did my best to breathe slowly and to silence the voice inside me that said I didn't belong in this depressing place, and that I was never going to, and that we never should have come here, and that my mother was mental.

The library did still exist, they said, but it was a long walk beyond the other side of Clanfedden Bridge and then an easy-to-miss turn to the left and then a steep mile up a narrow lane. I set off.

By the time I got there I was soaking and cold but there was light coming from within, and a car parked outside and two doors with CLANFEDDEN LIBRARY in a curve above them.

I pushed them open. They were the heavy, swinging kind.

'Welcome to Clanfedden library and post office,' said someone immediately, like she had been expecting me. She was standing behind a counter. Tall and old. Long nose. Twinkly eyes. She had a nametag pinned on her bobbly frayed jumper. *Veronica Grassbloom, Chief Librarian.*

'I'm very glad you found us. It is wonderful to see you.'

CHAPTER 5

For the first time since I'd arrived in this town, my skin didn't feel clammy and my heart stopped banging inside my chest. I liked Veronica Grassbloom straight away.

She asked me if I was a visitor. I told her yes, I was going to be here for a while.

'Fantastic!' she said. 'You've come at a most opportune time. The library committee is about to meet and we have several members about your age. I'm expecting some of them any minute. We're preparing for Clanfedden's annual book fair, three weeks from Thursday. This is its fourth year! I can hardly believe it. In any case, it's always huge fun. Get involved if you like! Or at the very least save the date! If you're still in town then, of course.'

I told her I'd certainly think about it.

'Excellent,' she said. 'And, while you're here, let me sign you up for membership. Now where on earth have those library forms got to?' she said, opening and closing the drawers under the desk.

'It's OK,' I said. 'Don't worry about it.'

'Oh no, I'll find them, don't you worry,' she insisted. 'They're around here somewhere. Once you've filled one out, you'll be able to use the *complete range* of available facilities.'

I looked around. As far as I could see, the place was tiny, and the books were old and there was only one computer.

'OK, thanks,' I said.

'Do you have a particular service in mind?' she asked, still rummaging.

'No,' I said. 'Not really.'

'Researching your ancestry perhaps, or downloading key archives from our digital repository?'

'Em, to be honest, I was just looking for somewhere I can use my phone.'

She laughed. 'I should have guessed, you young people with those gizmos and gadgets! Certainly – here's the code. Take as long as you like. But might I also be so bold as to recommend a book?'

Veronica Grassbloom held a book out with both hands, and there was something about how kind she looked with her arms out like that, which made my eyes swim unexpectedly blurry and I was mortified.

She whispered something to me then, or at least I

thought she did. 'I'm sure whatever's going on, it will eventually be OK.'

'Pardon?' I said.

'Things can seem frightful at a particular moment in time, but they get better. It will pass. Everybody needs help once in a while, especially if they've just arrived in a new place.' She gave my arm the smallest squeeze. 'And while I'm on the subject, may I say again how welcome you are to Clanfedden, how much I hope you will like it while you are here, and that if you are in need of any assistance whatsoever, you only have to ask.'

'OK, great. Thanks,' I said, glad I was managing to keep my voice steady. 'Actually, right now I really just need somewhere to sit.'

She smiled. 'There is plenty of room,' she said, and flung her hand out as if I needed to be shown.

I walked carefully towards a table, pulled out a battered chair. I took a breath, sat down and closed my eyes.

And I still remember that single moment of calm like an island in time. How cool and gentle it felt there in the silky quiet.

But soon the air churned with other sounds, human noises coming from the door. The staccato clicks of feet, the hiss of whispers, the roar of laughter, and then the three of them toppled in – two girls, one boy.

As soon as they saw me, they went quiet shushing and jostling and nudging each other and then sprawling, not far from me, in various shapes on the old soft ripped chairs, spreading themselves out the way friends who've known each other for ever do. I instantly compared myself to them, wishing I had that confidence, longing for the protection that comes with long-formed bonds.

The boy wore a brown polo neck, enormous glasses, skinny jeans. One of the girls was in green dungarees and had curly hair like a big mop. The other had long shiny plaits tied at the end with what looked like orange string. They stared at me. I looked away.

I came to the library to be on my own. I wasn't ready for people.

I moved to the table in the furthest away corner, plugged in my phone, shoved in my earphones, turned the music up and checked for messages. Needless to say, there were none except for the usual twenty from Tom, which I automatically deleted. I sat with my back to the three of them, staring at the wall.

It wasn't long before a soft, small object landed on my head, and then another.

Really? I thought, plucking the paper pellets out of my hair. I turned and glared. I could see the two girls tugging at the boy's arm.

'What's your problem?' I asked.

'What's yours?' the boy asked back.

'I don't have one.'

The girl with plaits kicked him, but you could see it was

one of those gentle kicks that friends like that give each other from time to time.

'Stop it, Conor,' she said.

'Right, OK, forget it,' I said, standing and getting ready to leave, but my headphones tangled around my backpack and my fingers were clumsy as sausages and my backpack fell off my shoulder, knocking a nearby stack of books to the floor.

I made it to the door, but Veronica Grassbloom was standing there, holding up an application form all triumphant like this was the best thing ever.

'I found one!' she declared.

She made me come back to the front desk to fill it out, wouldn't take no for an answer. I scribbled everything in as quickly as I could using a pencil that was tied to a string.

'Luca . . . Spinelli?' Veronica said, looking at my completed form.

'Yeah,' I said.

Something happened in her eyes. She stared into mine. It felt a little bit like torture.

'Oh, my. But this . . . this must mean the rumours are true! That she *is* back and that you are somehow related to her!'

She whispered my mother's name then. Ariana. Ariana Spinelli.

'Yes,' I sighed. 'Yes, I'm her son.'

The silence seemed to go on for ever as she kept looking at me and I kept looking at her.

'Ariana Spinelli's son,' she said at last. 'Well, goodness me, what a thing. I didn't believe it at first – it's been so long since she was here. But now. Well, well, well. My goodness me.'

Veronica handed me a library card. I glanced back at the three friends who were sitting at a table now, heads close together, watching me.

I mumbled a goodbye to Veronica and left.

Back on Main Street, I burst through our new front door like a punch.

My mother had her huge pink rubber gloves and overalls on and was standing on the very top of a stepladder pulling out rusty nails.

'Oh *amore*, hello! Did you find it?'

'Yes, I found it.'

'Ah, *bene!* Does it still smell of wood and chocolate? Is Veronica Grassbloom there? How was it?'

'It was dreadful, Mum,' I shouted. 'Every bit of it is dreadful. The library, the streets, this whole place.'

The banging and hammering all around us stopped. My mother's team of workers went silent. She clapped her hands, told them to take a break and climbed down the creaky ladder to face me.

'What is it, Luca? What's wrong?'

'What's wrong? What's *wrong*? Everything is. I haven't the faintest idea what we are actually doing here.'

'Oh, Luca,' my mother said, and she put her hands on my shoulders and pressed me gently into a paint-spattered chair.

'Mum, come on. Can't you admit you've made a mistake? Can't we just cut our losses and go back?'

'No, actually. No, we can't.'

'But you *told me*. You *said* we could go back whenever we wanted. You said every decision was reversible.'

'Well, I'm sorry, I was wrong.'

My mother had invested every single drop of her savings into this Clanfedden plan. She had used most of her money to buy this place and was using the rest from the sale of our old house to do it up.

'I know it is rather shabby and dirty right now, and I know you're feeling *un po' perso* but soon it is going to look fantastic, and – and well, everything is going to be wonderful.

'This is the time for our new start. No looking back. We have to dive in, heads first! Sometimes you simply have to burn your bridges.'

'You should have asked me.' My voice sounded strange and thin. 'You should have told me. You promised if I didn't like it, we wouldn't have to stay.'

She sat down and put her head in her hands so I couldn't see her face.

'Luca, you need to work with me here. We're supposed to be a team. We need to be in this together, or else . . .'

'Or else, what?'

She looked up at me then and there were tears wobbling in her eyes.

'Or else I don't know what I will do.'

'OK.' I took a deep breath. 'It's just that literally nothing in this place is anything like I expected it to be.'

She pulled her crumpled hankie out from under the folds of her overalls and blew her nose.

'E la vita, mi amore,' she replied, which roughly translated means *that's life* and was no help whatsoever.

'Please, Luca. Please. Will you give Clanfedden a chance?'

I got up without looking at her. I walked to the window and stared out onto the street trying to remember something I liked about my mother. Trying to remember that even though this whole move was crazier than anything she'd ever done, she'd mainly done it for me.

I began to help then, spending the next few hours sanding and clearing and sweeping and painting. And together with my mum and our team of builders, we made some progress.

The next day, in the middle of the afternoon there was an unexpected knock.

'Get that, will you, Luca?' shouted my mother from the top of her ladder.

I recognised the girl and her string-tied plaits straight away. This time I was able to look at her properly. Somehow without the scuffle and the embarrassment that had happened in the library, there were things I could see that I hadn't been able to see before. Honest eyes. Kind face.

'Hello.'

That was the first word Allie Redmond ever said to me.

It sounded like music.

PART 3

THE MIDDLE OF THE SUMMER

ALLIE REDMOND

CHAPTER 6

Luca Spinelli was a special kind of beautiful. Looking at his face that day in the library had been a puzzling experience, as if I was seeing a new colour that I'd never seen before, as if somebody was playing a joke or as if maybe he wasn't actually real. The moment he appeared was the exact moment when something important about my life started to shift. It felt like I was waking up after a very long sleep.

After he'd gone, the swinging doors flapping behind him, there was the smell of fresh mint in the air. I felt a bit dizzy.

I wouldn't have blamed him if he hated us. I was sure he probably did. I'd have hated us too.

I kept wishing Conor had decided on a different, more decent way to say hello, one that hadn't involved throwing paper at his head. *Why do my friends have to be such idiots*?

When Luca left, Conor and Poppy stared at each other for a second, and then in one movement leapt from the table we'd been sitting at, exploding into a joint scrabble, the two of them skating and sliding, a tangle of legs and arms, along the shining floorboards in a wordless dash towards the computer.

'OK, take it easy, please,' Veronica had said, coming over, her eyes all sparkly. 'What's this rush, in heaven's name?'

'Listen to her!' Poppy's voice was a shrill thread of amazement. 'Veronica, Veronica!' She held Veronica by the shoulders. 'This is an unprecedented event! There's a *new guy* in town. We're talking a totally new human being!'

'That's as may be,' smiled Veronica, 'but it isn't an emergency.'

'Of course it is!' said Poppy.

Obviously, Conor agreed. 'Yeah, at the very least, the guy needs to be googled without delay. That's what this library is for, isn't it, snooping on good-looking strangers?'

'Well no, actually it's not,' sighed Veronica. 'But if you must, then I suppose I can't stop you.'

If I'm honest, I was more curious about Luca Spinelli than anyone.

We clustered round the computer. As usual, Conor took charge, grabbing centre space, stretching his arms above him and then hovering his fingers out over the keyboard, a concert pianist about to begin a great concerto.

'Do you think Luca's spelled with a K or a C?'

'How many "L's" in *Spinelli*?'

There was a fizz in the air. We all felt it.

In a way it was kind of pathetic how excited we were.

Veronica watched us for a while, a resigned sort of expression on her face, and then she boiled the kettle, filled the old library teapot and got the biscuit tin out.

'Oh, sound! Tea and biscuits to sustain the research,' said Poppy.

We munched and sipped away, Poppy and Conor's faces shining in the light of the screen. Poppy's eyes were focused and big. Conor jiggled his foot the way he always does, full of the energy of anticipation.

None of us had a clue why anyone would want to move to Clanfedden. The last people who'd come here were Conor and his parents Brian and Pam, but that was a few years ago. We'd never expected to see anyone new now, not these days. Clanfedden had gone seriously downhill. The people here were twitchy and watchful. Nothing good or fun happened, with the possible exception of the book fair, and we only got excited about that because there was nothing else to get excited about. Every grown-up I'd ever met owed money to a guy called Jake McCormack. Jake McCormack more or less ran this town. There was hardly a place he didn't have some stake in. The Clanfedden Inn, buildings and property, farmland and fields, as far as you could see, and Crookthorpe House up on Crookthorpe Hill where he lived and where nobody except him ever went.

Just the sound of his truck approaching made little children cry and grown-up chins quiver. The mention of his name was enough to make a whole room go silent.

I didn't know what his face actually looked like, on account of how he always kept it covered with this black balaclava mask, but I could imagine it.

It was said that he had been burned in a fire once and was horribly mutilated and he had a frightening grin and a huge diagonal scar across his twisted face, jagged and glistening. He was supposed to have a glittering golden tooth that flashed like light on broken glass when he spoke.

His visits to the town were usually late at night. There wasn't a person in Clanfedden who didn't recognise the sound of that enormous clattery truck. Everyone knew the sight of those tyres – bigger than most people's cars. You could hear him coming for miles. My dad said it was terrible the way one man could have so much power.

Just before Luca came, there had been a recent snag in Jake's mission to control the town. It turns out that he did not own everything. Some of his business concerns were rented or leased. There were weak spots in his empire, my dad said, and the time had come to start doing something about it.

My dad had been the one to lead a petition of complaints about Jake's methods, particularly when it came to his betting and credit shop. It had been a long battle but finally they'd won. Dad and his community group had a big party the day they found out. There'd been speeches about how this was going to mark a new beginning for the town, and for a while, Dad seemed almost happy. But Conor told me Jake was furious about it, that this was not the beginning of anything. That everyone was going to regret it. When Jake McCormack was furious, everyone in the town was on higher alert than normal.

'Now all we need is someone to step up and buy the place,' Dad had said. And just as it seemed then that nobody would, especially after the menacing signs that Jake had told Conor's dad to put up in the window, the news came that somebody had put in an offer.

Jake McCormack knew about everything that went on in this town. He wielded his power like a weapon. He was the one in charge around here. People knew he was a dangerous man.

I knew it better than anyone.

I'm not sure why, but we assumed there'd be loads of information on Luca Spinelli. I suppose to us, he seemed exactly like the kind of city boy who would have a massive social media presence.

But the internet yielded literally nothing. Gradually, the rippling speed of Conor's keyboard clicks slowed to a dejected plod. Poppy's shoulders slumped.

'Wow,' she said. 'Nothing at all. That's unusual.'

'Yeah, kind of frustrating,' I agreed.

'And actually a bit weird, if you think about it,' said Conor, frowning.

We gazed at the computer some more, as if maybe by staring for long enough it might offer up some crumb of knowledge after all.

'Why don't you try Ariana,' suggested Veronica comfortingly. 'I'm quite sure there will be something about her.'

She was right, but then Veronica was always right. The first thing that came up was a paragraph from a newspaper article, written just that week. Poppy read it out using her presenter voice:

'Ariana Spinelli, one-time proprietor of the famed three-starred Cotto a Puntino *restaurant in Positano, Italy, has been quiet for almost half a decade. Rumours have swirled for years around her absence – the culinary scene has never been the same without her.*

'But now, that could all be about to change. Ariana Spinelli is back and she's planning to take Ireland's Mid-West region by storm. Sources say that a recent move to the sleepy town of Clanfedden, where she is said once to have lived, will mark the

beginning of a new phase in the professional life of this culinary genius.

The question on everyone's lips is: Will there be a new restaurant? That's under wraps for now. But critics and foodies alike are excited. Time will tell whether the rumours are true. Let's hope they are. With a chef this talented, it will certainly have been worth the wait.'

There was a photograph. Black eyes just like Luca's. Long, thick, wavy hair.

'What does three-star mean?' Poppy wondered.

Veronica's face was misty.

'The cooking world's finest prize,' she said, shaking her head. 'So she got her stars.'

We turned to her.

'I've tasted her food, you know.'

'What's she like?'

Veronica's eyes were dreamy and her voice had gone all soft and sort of velvety.

'Oh well, it's a long time ago now, and people change, but – well, she was like no one I'd ever met. And now she's back. I must admit, it is quite a mystery, quite a puzzle.'

We were hot with inquisitiveness but suddenly Veronica rapped a pencil on the counter.

'Right!' she said briskly. 'I've got work to do. Get off that computer, Conor Freeman. Enough chat. You have exhausted the internet with all that searching, and you've exhausted me with your questions. Remember what you're here for. We have preparations to make.' She pointed to the calendar behind our heads. 'There are only three weeks left. This book fair's not going to plan itself!'

We spent the rest of the afternoon drawing up schedules, moving stands around and painting posters, with Veronica directing like a conductor. Veronica had started the book fair the year Mum died. I often suspected she had done it for me. And in fairness to her it had always been a cheery day. She brought musicians from Limerick, and jugglers from Galway, and poets from Sligo and there were usually cupcakes topped with little fondant books nesting in whipped cream. Each of the three of us had important jobs. Organising readings, checking the stock of books, choosing the top ten novels for the children's club, blowing up the balloons, decorating the reception. For the month before the fair, it was practically our full-time job and Veronica wasn't wrong when she'd said there was still an awful lot to do.

For the whole afternoon, though, I was distracted and distant from the rest of them, and for the whole afternoon, that new minty fragrance floated in the air.

We walked home, saying goodbye to Conor on his side of the bridge and then like always, Poppy and I crossed the river and headed home along Main Street. That's when we saw Luca again. He didn't see us. He was busy standing in the window of Jake McCormack's shop, taking old paint off a wall with a scraper. Of course it wasn't Jake McCormack's any more. SOLD said a big sign outside it.

'Oh my God, it's them,' I said to Poppy, speeding up very fast so she had to run to keep up.

A slow chill began to travel through me like poisoned syrup. Luca and this mother probably knew nothing about the building they had bought. They didn't realise what they'd done. They didn't know that Jake McCormack basically owned this town.

Someone was going to have to warn them.

'What? What?' Poppy kept saying, running to keep up with me, clueless.

'The new boy Luca, the guy we met today and his mother Ariana. They're the ones who've bought Jake McCormack's place.'

'Oh.'

'We have to warn them,' I said. 'We have to let them know what the story is.'

'Why do we have to do that? It's none of our business,' said Poppy.

'When Jake McCormack has a claim on something, everyone needs to stay away from it. There isn't a person in Clanfedden who doesn't know this. Why do you think nobody from this town was interested in buying his shop?'

But Poppy was looking at her phone. Her mother had texted telling her dinner was ready.

'Gotta go, Al,' she said vaguely, skipping off.

If I didn't tell the Spinellis about Jake McCormack, I was afraid nobody would, and they'd be hounded by him for the rest of their lives.

As soon as I got home, I rang Veronica and told her the news.

'My goodness me,' she said.

'Exactly,' I said. 'Don't you think someone should tell them?'

'Yes, yes, of course, I do,' she replied. 'Would you like me to say something?'

'No, Veronica, it's fine. I just wanted to make sure you thought it was OK for me to. I'm nearer and you're so busy. I'll to call into them tomorrow and explain everything. Maybe they'll be able to get out of the place before they've wasted too much time and energy on it.'

'Darling Allie,' said Veronica, 'you are some girl. Always looking out for other people.'

But the truth was, it was Veronica, who did the most looking out for people in this town. She cared about everyone. She cared especially about me.

CHAPTER 7

Very few people knew the whole story, but for a long time, Veronica Grassbloom had been my sanity and my safety. I used to call her my second mother. Though I stopped calling her that in the end, because calling someone else your second mother seems a wrong and dark thing to do after your first one has actually died.

Veronica was my go-to person in Clanfedden. When my mum got sick, Veronica was the only one who never lost hope. She was the one who kept cheerful and tried her best to be positive for my mum when everyone else – even my dad – had given up. I was never going to forget that.

The library became like another home to me, which was fairly handy seeing as my actual home had become a cold and awkward place where I never usually wanted to be.

Veronica believed in a simple life, she told me once,

living in a flat in the library's basement, growing much of her own food in the allotment behind the car park.

I knew how much she had quietly looked out for me over the years, especially after my mum died.

With her bobbly jumper and messy hair and her often-untied shoelaces and her glasses held together with Sellotape, she wasn't the kind of person to go looking for attention.

I could trust her with anything. She never got annoyed, not even with Conor or Poppy, who spent most of their library visits squeaking and laughing and clattering around the place like two elephants.

I sometimes went to the library just to sit there and feel her kindness floating around in the air. You could tell she was on my side – handing me snacks if I needed them, silently placing a bundle of books beside me, asking me how I was doing. She always told me that if things ever got bad, she was the one I could go to for help. That she would always be here. If the library was closed, I could just bang on the door of the basement and she would appear. This was a comforting thing. It got me through a lot of dark days. Like the day Dad sat in the living room with the curtains closed and wouldn't say a word. And the first Mother's Day after Mum had died, when even the calendar felt like a cruel thing.

But probably what was most important about Veronica and me is that we shared a secret. A secret about a terrible, stupid thing I once did. She helped to get me out of it. I'd only been a kid at the time, but if it wasn't for Veronica, that mistake could have followed me around for a long time.

I owed her everything.

It was a dark January just after my tenth birthday that we found out Mum's treatment wasn't going to fix her after all. The doctors told us they'd tried everything but there are times, they said, when everything doesn't work. According to them, there was nothing more they could do.

In those days, I thought Dad could fix anything, but then overnight, there were things he could not fix. Apparently we were supposed to stop hoping for a miracle because no miracle was coming. I remember I went kind of crazy. I hit Dad in the chest with my fists, and I screamed at the doctors and the nurses and told them how useless they were.

They were going to have to be patient with me, Dad explained to the medical team, on account of me being so full of grief and desperation. Eventually I calmed down but when we were on our own at home and when the doors were closed, I started to do my research.

We brought Mum home the next day. *Home to spend her last weeks in her own environment*, Dad said, which I hated him for, obviously.

They said I should feel free to chat to her as much as I could even when she was sleeping.

'Don't worry, Mum,' I whispered. 'I'm not going to let you die. I promise I'm not.'

I found out about a treatment that you could buy online that other people had got brilliant results from and I read testimonials from real people saying how they had been cured. It was going to cost a lot of money but I was sure when I showed it to Dad that he'd find a way.

'Allie, love, please stop this,' is what he actually said when I did show it to him.

He wouldn't even give it a try. He tried to explain things to me, things I did not understand, things I could not believe. So then my stupid ten-year-old brain starts thinking, 'If Dad won't help me, I'm just going to do this on my own.'

Dad banned me from using the internet after that, which is how I'd ended up in the library. It was Veronica who had seen me searching and had asked if she could help. I told her what I needed. I said there was medicine for Mum that might work. I said I had no money and she sighed and said she'd do anything to help, especially because this was Rachel we were talking about.

The only place she knew where money could be got quickly was from someone like Jake McCormack, and he was a dangerous man and of course we couldn't do that.

I begged her to go to him for me. At first she said no.

'You have to understand who you'd be dealing with, Allie. If you cross him, or if you owe him, he'll go after you. That man gets entertained by other people's distress. He enjoys seeing people in pain. It gives him a kind of a thrill. Jake McCormack takes what he wants, and he maims before he kills. It's in his nature. He enjoys watching people scared and suffering.'

I begged her some more, telling her there was nobody else I could turn to, and in the end, it was her kind heart that relented. In the end she said yes, she would help me, because these were desperate times. I could see the worry in her eyes, but I didn't care. As a matter of fact, I was kind of elated, because like I said, I was a stupid little kid who hadn't a clue about anything.

I set up a bank account in Mum's name – it was easier than I thought it would be, and Veronica helped, even though the whole time she kept saying, 'Oh, Allie, this all feels quite wrong.' But I kept her focused. 'Don't fail me now, Veronica. I need you.'

Soon the money was in the account and I was able to pay for the medicine online and fifteen hundred euros might seem like a lot of money but not when it comes to a chance of life instead of certain death.

The medicine arrived in a gigantic padded envelope. The postman couldn't fit it in the letterbox so he rang our doorbell. Dad answered.

There were lots of questions then, of course.

'What on earth is this all about?'

I didn't want to get Veronica into trouble, but in the end he got everything out of me. And then I said, 'Let's not worry about the details, let's just start giving this to Mum, now that it's here. It stands an excellent chance of making her better.'

And when I said that, he hugged me for ages and ages, as if that was going to help our situation in any way.

He brought me to the library. He held me by the hand. He was very cross with Veronica. I felt terrible, but Veronica was great about it. She said she understood. She said she was dreadfully sorry. She knew that this had been an awful thing to do, and she didn't know what had possessed her, and she began to cry.

'I don't know, Rory, it's just she came to me, and I had to do something – for her and for you and for Rachel,' she said.

And Dad said, 'Oh, Vonnie, come on now, don't cry, I'm sorry I upset you like this.'

In the end even Dad agreed the medicine might be worth a try. Nothing to lose. Veronica came round most evenings to see Mum and she helped us out too, me and Dad. And there was a while when we had hope again.

But that didn't last very long.

*

Dad said he was glad her death had been a gentle one. He claimed that we were going to get comfort from that. And we forgot about Jake McCormack and I forgot about everything, and there are a few weeks that are just a smudgy blur in my head.

It wasn't long before the phone calls from Jake began. I remember the first.

'My mother is dead,' I told him.

'Yes, well, sorry for your troubles and all that but there is money owed.'

I could hear the noise of his breath.

Jake would not stop ringing and soon the amount of money we owed had for some reason been multiplied by four. Dad had stopped answering the phone. If I didn't answer it, I knew Jake would ring and ring and ring.

'This is what your mother signed up to,' Jake said. 'She should have read the small print.'

My mother hadn't signed up to anything. It was me who had brought this on us.

'To tell you the truth,' he said, 'I'm getting sick of waiting. You can give your father a message from me: if he doesn't pay his wife's debt by the end of this week, there is going to be trouble. Very bad trouble.'

The way Jake had said 'very bad trouble' made me sure that the trouble he was talking about was full of violence and pain and destruction. And if there'd been any room for doubt, Jake went on: 'Tell him I'll destroy him. Tell him he'll have a lifetime of new problems if he doesn't make me his number one priority.'

He wouldn't stop. He rang over and over again and his gravelly voice would rasp threats down the phone. 'Bad things will happen,' he said.

'Bad things have already happened,' I said to him.

'You don't know what you're letting yourself in for,' he replied.

I practically ran up the library lane to Veronica after that, and when I got there I practically fell through the doors.

'It's that Jake McCormack, isn't it?' she said immediately, before I had said a word.

'Yes,' I gasped. 'The debt is getting bigger every day. If he doesn't get his money, something bad is going to happen. He said so. He won't stop ringing.'

I remember how Veronica's knuckles had sharpened and whitened and how her face went tight.

'Oh, that man,' she said, her lips trembling. 'That nasty, horrible, greedy man.'

I remember the hiss of a pulled tissue from the box on the counter and how Veronica had closed her kind arms around me.

'I have savings, my dear girl,' she soothed, 'and I feel so responsible for this. I am going to pay Jake McCormack the money he is looking for.'

She came round that evening.

'I've called that rotten man off,' she told Dad. 'The debt is gone. You won't be getting any threats from Jake McCormack any more.'

'We owe you so much,' Dad said.

'Not in the slightest,' she replied. 'I'm glad to have been able to help. I just wish I could have helped Rachel too.'

That night we put music on in the kitchen and Dad smiled for the first time in ages.

Veronica visited a lot after that. But one day in the living room I saw her leaning close to Dad, saying something very quiet. He looked sad. And I don't know exactly what they'd been talking about, but after that Veronica didn't come back to our house again, which was a pity.

So in the end there wasn't much comfort to be got from anywhere. Mum had died, and Veronica no longer called, and even though the debt was gone, I couldn't stop dreaming of Jake. And in my dreams, I could see things that you can't see in real life. I was able to see Jake McCormack's horrible face smiling a terrible twisted smile, and when I woke I stayed blinded for a second by the echo of the glint of his golden tooth and by the jagged lines of his glistening scars.

And somehow, even after Veronica had made everything better, the thought of Jake McCormack kept haunting me.

I told Dad about my dreams and he squeezed his fingers into two shaking fists.

'Someone needs to stop that man,' he said. 'He may not be hounding us any more, but Jake McCormack is terrorising the town. That's all he's ever done. It's not right. Someone needs to stop him.'

CHAPTER 8

Poppy: 'When are we heading to the library?'

Allie: 'Can't go today,'

Poppy: 'Ah why?'

Allie: 'There's just this thing I have to do, so see you tomorrow, K?'

Poppy: 'OK, then, mystery woman.'

When I made it to Main Street the next day, Jake McCormack's place already looked different. Everything had been washed clean and bright. The door had been sanded down and there was a smooth feel to it when I knocked.

Luca was the one who opened the door.

'Hello,' I said.

'Hello,' he said back, smiling and I just stood staring at him like a fool and there was this big long silence.

This is how I filled it:

'OK, firstly, I mean, em, I meant to ask you, would you be interested in joining the library committee? We meet in the library. The other two aren't as bad as they seem.'

'I'll think about it,' he replied, looking into my eyes. 'But I'm going to be kinda busy helping out with this place,' he added.

What a stupid opening line. Of course he wasn't going to join the library committee, especially not after the way Conor had behaved.

We stood for another while then.

'Listen,' I said. 'There's something else. Would you mind if . . . I mean, is there any chance . . . I wonder if I could say hello to your mother, if she's here? There's something I need to talk to you both about.'

'Yeah, sure,' he said cheerfully. 'I'll get her. Come on in.'

I took a step inside. It felt weird being there. I looked at the walls and the giant cans of paint. I heard footsteps coming down the stairs, and soon she was walking towards me, her hair flowing, a clinking necklace with stones of bright blue and pale saffron yellow.

'Hello, em. Hello,' I said as she approached.

'Oh, goodness me, hello hello,' she said. 'Who are you?'

'My name is Allie Redmond.'

'Come on in. Would you like some tea?'

We sat, Ariana, Luca and me, all in a row on this big

orange sofa and even then while the place was still being fixed up and painted, there was a feeling of welcome that I could almost feel on my skin, like warmth or sunshine.

Before I could say much else, straight away, she began asking me about myself, my school, my parents. It's always horrible when people do that, because there's no way around the truth.

'Yeah, I live on Clanfedden Drive with my dad. My mum died.'

Most adults who I say this to will mumble some hurried words of sympathy and then quickly start talking about something else, but Ariana stared at me.

'Oh, my dear. And, do you mind if I ask you, how long ago did she die exactly?'

'Four years.'

She placed her hand on my arm.

'What was her name?'

'Her name was Rachel,' I said, not being able to avoid the small crack in my voice that sometimes happens when I say her name.

'Rachel? Rachel Reilly?'

'Yeah, I mean that what she was before she married my dad. She was Rachel Redmond after that.'

Ariana came even closer to me and before I could stop her, she put her hands on my face, and she said, 'Oh dear,' and '*mi Dio*.'

Then huge diamondy tears fell down her face and she

just let them fall and she didn't apologise the way people normally do when they start crying randomly in front of a stranger. And it was pretty much the weirdest feeling in the world.

She fished a blue-and-white hankie from her dress and she wiped her tears and then she said:

'Your mother. Your mother. I loved her so much. Thank you for coming. I'm so glad you've called to say hello.'

'How did you know her?' I asked, feeling kind of sick.

'The most wonderful seven summer holidays of my life, here in Clanfedden when I was a teenager. She and I became friends because we both played tennis, but of course she was always so much better than me! And I taught her to cook. She was talented and funny. My best friend in the world. My heart broke when I heard she had died.'

She paused then as if something was occurring to her for the first time. 'Oh my darling, I am so sorry. Your loss, your grief, the hole that there must be.'

I suppose it should have been great to meet someone who'd known and loved my mother, but I hadn't been expecting anything like this. I'd come to give Ariana a message, I'd come to warn her. And suddenly I didn't want to be there at all. I didn't want to talk about my mother any more because if I did, the old sadness was going to drown me.

I'd had a reason for calling, and this was not it.

'Look, it's great to hear, and it's nice to meet you, and

I'm glad you knew my mum and everything, but I need you to listen. This place you have bought. There is something about it that you need to know.'

'What is it?'

'There's a man in this town. He considers the shop to be his. It doesn't do to get on the wrong side of him. He put up signs to say that nobody should attempt to buy the place or there will be trouble.'

'I have seen those signs myself, my dear,' she smiled.

'But . . .'

'It is so good of you to have come to tell me this . . .' Ariana continued kindly and she did seem really grateful. She stroked my hair. 'I can see it of course, the more I look at you: so very like your mother. Thank you, lovely girl.'

Luca wasn't saying a word. All this time he just sat there listening.

'No problem. You're welcome. Glad to be of use. So you'll move then? You'll find another place?' I said.

'Whatever gave you that idea?' She laughed. 'Of course not! You needn't have troubled yourself. The very nice man who worked here, Brian Freeman, has already told me everything there is to know. He has been here to advise me to desist, believing us to have been unwise. He too says it is an inadvisable thing we have done. But no one must worry. Ariana Spinelli is prepared. Ariana Spinelli is unafraid!'

'There was a funeral, you know,' I said. 'For Mum.'

'I am sorry. I was far away in Positano and we had lost touch. I didn't know.'

I covered my face with my hands for a few seconds, but then, worried that I was making an idiot of myself, I took them away again.

'I didn't mean to upset you. Please, Allie, stay for another while. If you have time. I could answer your questions and you could answer mine.'

I couldn't imagine there being any circumstances that would make me want to stay for another second, not even with Luca sitting there. I'd come to warn them. That was it. I'd done my human duty. But if Conor's dad hadn't been able to persuade her, then what chance did I have?

'I have no questions to ask or to answer. I just wanted you to know about McCormack,' I said. 'I have to go now.'

'I'll see you to the door,' said Luca, but I could barely speak. 'I'm sorry about my mum,' he said.

'It's OK,' I answered. I realised I'd left my phone on the sofa.

Luca went back to get it. But before he gave it to me he said: 'Here, will I put in my number, you know, em . . . just in case?'

'Yeah,' I said. 'Yeah, OK.'

I unlocked it for him and he punched in his number, his head bent over my screen, his face serious. The sadness was coming like a huge wave. I grabbed my phone out of his hand. I don't think I even said goodbye. I jogged down Main Street, and in the end I ran and I kept on running fast and kind of crazy until I got home, as if there really was a big wave and as if it was coming for me.

I went straight to my room and I took the photo of my mother down off the wall. I looked at it for a long time.

'I never knew you played tennis,' I said to the photo as if she was still alive. 'I never knew you had a friend called Ariana Spinelli. How come you never told me?'

Dad popped his head in to see if I was OK. I told him I'd met Ariana. He sat down at the end of my bed, which he hadn't done for a long time.

'Was Mum really her best friend?'

'Oh, well, your mum had many best friends. But yes, they were very close, long ago.'

'Did you know that Ariana was back in Clanfedden?'

'I had heard.'

'Did you know she's bought Jake McCormack's place?'

'Yes, I heard that too. And I think it's a good thing, Allie. Good that that man's business will be gone, and there'll be something new and different there from now on, and we'll be able to forget about him altogether. It's brilliant news for Clanfedden really, when you think about it.'

I told him about meeting Ariana's son Luca, and about

calling in on them and about how weird it was to hear that Ariana knew so much about Mum, but had never even seen her when she was sick. My dad didn't say anything.

For a second, I wanted him to plump up my pillow, the way he used to do or laugh his old laugh. I wanted to tell him how worried and strange I suddenly felt, but there was no pillow plumping and there was no laughter and I did not tell him any of the things that were in my head. He just clicked the door closed and I could hear his heavy footsteps plodding slowly down our stairs.

That night I woke to a strange red glow filling my room. I got up and opened my curtains.

A great burning ball of red light hovered over the centre of town. I could see swirls of fire tumbling upwards into the sky over Main Street.

Something wild was happening. Bad things were coming.

CHAPTER 9

Dad threw on his dressing gown and put on his slippers and we ran to the car and he drove to Main Street. We weren't the only ones. People had seen the smoke and the blaze from miles around. Everyone had come to help.

Luca and Ariana had rescued themselves. They hadn't been hurt. They'd both walked out of the burning building without a scratch or a singe.

'The secret is always to stay calm,' Ariana was explaining to the gathered crowd by the time we got there. She was holding an old book in her arms like it was a baby.

Luca was shaking people's hands, saying, 'Thank you.'

'It is so good of you all to have come,' said Ariana.

Fintan Brown wrapped blankets round their shoulders, and it was only when Delilah Scully placed a mug of hot chocolate into Luca's hands that I noticed he was shaking slightly.

I hurried over to him.

'Oh my God, Luca. Are you OK?'

Luca said he was grand. They both were.

'It must have been the electrical wires in the place,' Ariana said. 'My builders were telling me only the other day that they were faulty and old and in need of repair.'

'What an awful thing!' said Alice Morrison, and Ariana agreed, seeming quite unruffled, cheerful even.

'I'm just relieved that it wasn't worse,' she explained. 'It's better it happened now rather than later. It would have been a great deal more disastrous if the whole place had been kitted out!' She smiled. 'We'll have the place right again in no time!'

I stood close to Luca and whispered to him, 'Luca, listen, I'm so glad you're OK and your mum. But can't you see, the things I told you yesterday. You need to understand what's going on here.'

But by then the adults were deciding loudly that everyone better go home and back to bed. It had been agreed that Ariana and Luca were to stay the night with Tina and Ciara Marshall.

Everything was going to be fine, people kept saying. There'd been no damage to human life, which was the main thing, and the engines had come quickly and the fire was out. The rest of the clean-up could wait until the morning. How admirable it was that Ariana and Luca had never panicked. How amazed everyone was by their humour and good natures, even in an emergency of this kind.

'But you must realise,' I pleaded. 'You must realise who did this.'

Nobody else said anything except Dad, and all he said was, 'Come on, Allie, now.'

And he hurried me back into the car before I could even say goodbye to Luca.

At home, I did not go back to sleep. I thought about Jake McCormack – of what he'd just done and of his greed and his power and his vicious, jealous ways, and I felt as frightened as I'd ever felt.

Early next morning I texted Luca.

'Listen, Luca, I know it's terrible what happened, but the one good thing is that maybe now would be the time to persuade your mum to start looking for a different building, just like I tried to suggest.'

'DON'T WORRY! IT'S ALL GOING TO BE FINE. MY MOTHER MAY SEEM A LITTLE ODD BUT SHE HAS A VERY GOOD BUSINESS HEAD, AND BESIDES THERE IS INSURANCE. THE PLACE WILL BE FIXED UP AGAIN IN NO TIME.'

By the time I showed up to the library the next day, Conor and Poppy had reorganised the whole place. There were posters all over the outside and preparations for the fair were looking better than they had. Veronica waved at me from the counter.

Poppy wanted to know if the Spinellis were going to change their plans now that there had been a fire.

I told them the Spinellis were had no intention of changing their plans, that they weren't going to move anywhere. Nobody mentioned Jake McCormack.

Veronica shook her head. 'She's amazing,' she said. 'Nothing's going to stand in that extraordinary woman's way, not even her building being set on fire.'

'How did it happen?' asked Conor, and before I could say anything, Veronica clapped her hands together very loudly and said there were still at least a hundred jobs that needed to be done. She'd drawn up a list.

I sat on the edge of one of the small library seats by the window and stared out at the street. I couldn't move. That terrible chill was rippling through me again.

Veronica placed her kind hand on my shoulder.

'What is it?' she asked quietly.

'It's the fire last night,' I said simply. 'I'm worried, Veronica. I'm worried about what Jake McCormack's going to do next.'

She looked surprised. 'Well, goodness me, what's Jake McCormack got to do with it?'

'Veronica, come on, please – not you too. Isn't it obvious? He wants the Spinellis out of his shop. He'll stop at nothing.'

'Oh no, Allie. Of course I can see why you might think that, but honestly, I don't think there's any evidence that anyone started last night's fire on purpose.'

'But how can you be sure?'

'I've been talking to Conor's dad about it. There were faulty electrics. He feels terrible not to have told the Spinellis about the bad wiring. But that's all it was. Really, Allie, you mustn't worry.'

Veronica was never usually wrong about anything but I knew she was wrong now. I knew everyone was.

'They're going to go ahead with their plan,' I said. 'The fire hasn't changed anything, and by the way how come nobody told me she was a friend of Mum's?' I said. 'Did you know?'

'I did,' said Veronica.

'Why didn't you tell me?' I asked.

'Your mother was very sad when they lost touch,' Veronica said, hesitating a bit. 'And Allie, I don't wish to speak ill of anyone, but Ariana Spinelli – well, she is a wonderful woman in so many ways but I understand she may not have been the most loyal of your mother's friends.'

'What do you mean?'

'Oh well, it's been such a long time. Long, long before you were born, long, long before your mum was ever ill. We were only your age when Rachel and I first met her. Summer after summer Ariana visited. We even gave a party for her on her birthday, her twenty-first. The whole town came. But then one summer, suddenly, she stopped coming.

'Just disappeared. I gather there was some falling out of some kind between her and Rachel.' She smiled then. 'When people are young everything feels so much more dramatic. I'm sure it was a small thing or perhaps nothing at all. Just gossip.'

I wanted to ask lots of other questions then but Conor and Poppy were shouting 'Allieeeeee, Alllieeee,' like there was some big emergency over in the other corner of the library, which there was not.

'Dad's stressed out of his head,' Conor told us. 'Says McCormack's furious. And Dad's thinks he'll be out of a job soon which means he's going to be broke and we're probably not going to be able to go on holiday now, and there goes any chance of any pocket money ever again for the rest of my natural life.'

'Oh no,' I said.

'Dad says the Spinellis are up to no good. He's heard they are a scheming pair. And you know something? I can't help thinking about the way Luca behaved the other day up here – kinda snobby. Like he thinks he's better than us.' Poppy was nodding.

'What makes you say that?' I said.

'Yeah, remember the way he practically told us to flip off?' added Poppy, a new, vinegary kind of tone in her voice.

'Bit strange,' said Conor. 'All we did was say hello . . .'

'Would the two of you shut up please? I'm not having this,' I interrupted.

'Why?'

'Because these are lies, the things you've just said. You didn't say hello to him and he never told you to flip off. He wasn't rude. Not even the slightest bit. If anything, it's *you* who were horrible to *him*. Throwing those paper pellets at his head as if you were six, and that aggressive way you talked to him. The only thing he did was get up and leave. And you can't blame him for that. Anybody else would have done the same.'

'Oooh, touchy touchy,' said Conor.

After that I just left it. I hated fighting with either of them.

We spent the rest of the morning hanging decorations and printing cardboard bookmarkers and setting display tables. Conor and Poppy kept giving me instructions that I didn't hear or if I did, I kept getting wrong.

'You are a basket case today, really you are,' scolded Poppy.

'Yeah, I know,' I said.

My phone pinged.

'Are you free later? And would you like to hang out?' said the text. It was from Luca.

I realised, with a strange flip of my heart, that there was nothing I would like more.

CHAPTER 10

Luca Spinelli and I ended up in the playground at seven thirty that night, both of us wobbling around on each of the two grimy old swings beside the buckled seesaw.

We talked about a lot of things. We stayed there for ages.

I tried to explain again about how the fire was definitely not an accident, how it was obviously Jake McCormack, and Luca said, 'Listen, Allie, I appreciate your concern, both me and my mother do, but the thing is, my mother simply won't countenance this kind of talk. It would be better if you left it.'

'But there are so many things you and your mother don't understand about Clanfedden. I wanted to make sure you were fully in the picture.'

'Yeah, and that's so decent of you, but the thing is, my mum's not worried about Jake McCormack.'

'What do you mean?'

'She thinks he's a coward. She doesn't know why people are so scared of someone who won't show their face, who lurks around in the dark, who won't stand up and be counted.'

I couldn't blame him for not understanding.

'Luca, your mum is wrong. The guy has awesome power.'

'Does he live in Clanfedden?'

'No, he lives high up there.' I pointed to the dark forest way, way up. 'It's called Crookthorpe Hill. Do you have a bike?'

He said he did.

'Well, if you like we could cycle up there one day together and I could show you.'

'Em, thanks anyway, but no thanks,' he said.

'I thought you said you weren't scared of him.'

'I'm not scared of *him,*' Luca replied, looking up at the Crookthorpe trees, 'I'm scared of *heights.*'

He'd already seen the road to Crookthorpe Hill, he said. He'd been told how sharply the ledges on that top road dropped into the valley.

'Mortally afraid. They make me faint. And now that you know my darkest secret, you have to tell me yours.'

'I don't have a dark secret,' I said, and he said fair enough.

Instead we talked about music and Netflix and books and school and our favourite subjects and to be honest, I can't even remember everything we said that night. But talking to him felt comfortable and surprising, surreal and familiar all in one.

Then there was a funny empty moment when the swings went still and all I could hear was the small creak of their rusty chains. I said how weird it was that our mothers had been best friends once and he agreed.

'Allie,' he said. 'I'm really sorry your mum is dead. That's so lousy.'

It was like the wind had been taken out of my lungs. Until yesterday, no one had mentioned her for a long time. Most people acted like they had forgotten. Sometimes it felt as if she'd never been here at all.

It had been a strange thing to hear his mum talking about a time when my mum was young and strong, when her sickness had not cast its horrible shadow across our lives. I told him how my own memories of her had been pretty much wrecked by what she'd had to go through before she died. I told him how I hated the idea of my mother being weak and frail, but that any time I thought about her, this is what I remembered.

Luca stood up and walked over to me. He put his hand on my hand and he didn't ask a question or make a statement or give advice. He just said my name twice, very quietly.

And the sadness in me swelled like a dark ocean. I wanted to say a million things to him. To thank him for listening. I wanted to hang on to his hand, to hug him, to kiss his cheek even. But I was afraid if I did any of those things, the feelings and memories inside me might spill out in frightening, maybe dangerous ways, so instead I did the thing I always do when I feel deep and intense things like that; I changed the subject.

'Why the heck would anybody want to move here?'

Luca shrugged and smiled a little, and sat back down on his swing.

Levering with his feet, he twisted the chain above him around and around. Then he let go, spinning himself into a colourful blur.

'It wasn't really my idea,' he said, once he had slowed down. 'It was my mother's. It was mainly a business decision. That, and a whole load of romantic memories she has about this town.'

We wobbled towards each other. Our faces moved very close. I could feel the warmth of him.

A huge loud noise burst into the air, giving me a fright. It was Luca's phone. He fished it from his pocket and stared at it. It kept on ringing.

'Aren't you going to get that?'

'Nope.'

'Why not?'

'Because I know who it is.'

With a sort of flourish he pressed the red button. Two minutes later the ringing began again and again two minutes after that.

'Pretty keen, whoever they are,' I said.

And Luca said, 'I'd much rather keep talking to you,' in a way that made my face go hot.

We couldn't stay there all night.

'Luca, I'm really glad you've come to Clanfedden. I can't get over that you and your mum are going to stick it out and stay with the plan even though your place was nearly burned to the ground. I'm really glad you texted me. I'm really glad we've had this chat.'

'Same,' he said, straight and honest. 'I think we're going to be friends,' he said.

'Yeah,' I said, 'I think so too.'

'Do you?' he replied, sounding slightly amazed. 'Great, OK, fantastic. But first you have to pass a test.'

I frowned.

'No, seriously. It's compulsory,' he said.

'OK. What kind of test is it?'

'A guess test.'

'Right, shoot.'

'Who do you say would win in a fight between the Hulk and a lion?'

'The Hulk? A lion? How would I know?'

'I'm not asking you to know; I'm asking you to guess. That's the whole point.'

I swung around in a spin myself, pretending to do some calculations in my head. I looked up at the darkening sky. I went for the Hulk.

'Hmm,' came his response. 'Interesting.'

'Did I guess right?' I asked, but he wouldn't say.

I'm not sure why, but I didn't feel like going to the library, and every time Conor or Poppy texted about it, I made some excuse or other. I kept meeting Luca in the playground, the next day and the day after that, and we'd always sit on the swings like we had the first time. A few nights later, Conor and Poppy found us there.

'Hi,' I said and, 'hi,' they said back but they didn't smile and they did not stop and I discovered I didn't care that much. There was a time when I would have cared a lot.

I couldn't stop thinking about the Spinellis – how nothing seemed to faze them, how they would not be intimidated or daunted, not by raging fires, not by the broken dirty streets, not by Jake McCormack.

And I could not stop thinking about how Ariana had known my mother well and loved her greatly, and how she knew things that I did not know – like, for example, my mum was a wonderful tennis player and until Ariana came, I'd never seen a photo of Mum in a white tennis dress with a shocking-pink lining that Ariana said flashed like rosy lightning every time she returned a ball, and how powerful and athletic and strong she had been. And it felt somehow as if those new stories had the power to take away other things I didn't want to think about. It was as if they could rub out the pictures I had of my mum in my head – pictures of her in bed, small and stooped and curled and sore and sick.

'Why did you never tell me that Mum played tennis?' I asked Dad, and maybe it came out angrier than I'd meant it to but anyway he practically shouted back that he couldn't be depended on to remember everything, and I shouted back, 'Too right, yeah, I forgot – you can't be depended on for lots of things.'

I didn't even know what I'd meant by that, but by then Dad and I were used to having conversations that always ended like this.

The rage hadn't started in our house until after Mum's funeral. Sometimes you'd hardly notice it, but other times, it filled up the whole house, so that it barely felt like there was room for anything else. It was like a separate force that roamed around, not belonging particularly to Dad or to me, but likely, at any random moment, to occupy one or other of us or, at the worst of times, to possess us both together simultaneously.

It seemed to prowl – like a scorpion maybe, or a panther, lurking under the stairs or sitting quietly on the couch, and then out of nowhere, for no good reason that I could see, pouncing, making us shout at each other and bang doors or say horrible, livid, non-retractable things.

The summer Mum died, I lost the gladness that used to be part of me. It was the year I became vigilant and silent, always anxious, never sure when things were going to kick off in me, or in Dad, or in us both.

Dad had been brilliant when she was alive. He was always solving problems, always fixing things that were broken, always good-natured and full of certainty and high spirits. It's not like it happened overnight, but after she died, very gradually, I could see those lovely things about him were disappearing.

He became slow to repair stuff, unwilling to answer the phone, quick to snap at me for doing things I hadn't even done. And he got properly angry for the smallest, stupidest reasons, for things that in the old days he'd never have noticed. Like when I forgot to lock the door when he was out, or when I left the fridge open or balanced a knife across a jar of jam. There was nothing I could do about the darkness that had grown inside him. At first I tried, but in the end I stopped.

I knew a big part of it was my fault. Even in the worst of arguments Dad never said he blamed me but it was obvious he was still angry about the money I'd borrowed, the foolish way I'd brought the threat of Jake McCormack down on us at the time when it had been the very last thing we'd needed.

He didn't have to say it, but I knew he'd never forgive me for that. I was just going to have to get used to it.

CHAPTER 11

It turns out that Conor had a cousin who had a friend whose brother went to Ashfield, which is the school that Luca had gone to before he came to Clanfedden.

Conor and his cousin got chatting one weekend on Instagram, and Conor had seen a picture of Luca, just an ordinary school photo in an Ashfield uniform, and he said, *Hey, that's Luca Spinelli. That guy lives in Clanfedden now.* And that's when Conor's cousin told Conor that his friend's brother had said Luca Spinelli had been expelled. Over something that had happened on a school trip. There weren't any more details than that.

It was obvious Conor had been dying to tell me because we hadn't talked in days and now there were five missed calls on my phone from him. I wished I hadn't called him back. I hated the way there was such sureness in his voice, and I hated the way I could hear Poppy's too, all smug in the background. I couldn't stand it.

After that, I started avoiding them even more purposely. It seemed like every single time I did meet them, they managed to get some dig or other in about Luca. How he was on the run. How he'd definitely done something bad in Dublin. How he and his mother would never have moved here if he hadn't burned his bridges in the city.

And I suppose it was only natural that in the end I asked Luca about it – about what those bridges might have been and how he might have burned them. He refused to say anything.

'Allie, please don't ask me to talk about my past, about what happened. I just can't do it.'

There was a shiver in his voice and a setting of his jaw that made me drop the subject.

Conor and Poppy became different after that. Their faces sterner, their heads higher. But even so, there were only so many days of silence that Poppy could ever tolerate before breaking the spell. She texted in the end to say it was ridiculous and that she and Conor were calling over. I said grand, no problem just as long as she knew that Luca was planning to call in too. But Conor and Poppy arrived before him. Conor wandered in, all slow and there was a terrible awkwardness in the air.

'Where have *you* been, stranger?' he asked.

'Oh, you know, busy, just hanging out.'

'Yeah,' said Conor, ambling around the living room and leaning against the back of the sofa with his arms crossed. 'Well, the reason we've called is that Veronica still has loads of things for us to do before the book fair. Are you going to show up to any of the meetings or have you packed it in or what?'

I'd sort of forgotten all about the fair.

'There's only ten days left now,' said Poppy. 'Like, this is countdown time.'

Normally I'd be the one rounding everyone else up.

'Look, guys,' I said. 'The thing is, I'm not sure if I can help out with the fair any more.'

'You're not sure you can help?' Poppy repeated, astonished. 'Allie, this is our thing. We're a team. You're totally letting us down if you back out now. We're heading up to the library this second as a matter of fact, and you really need to come with us.'

I wanted to say no. I wanted to say, *Guys, for your information there's a ton of other things going on for me right now.*

There was a knock on the door, and I knew it was Luca because we had a code. Three fast taps. Two slow ones.

'She's busy,' said Conor, staring at Luca, who had pushed the door open. 'She's coming to the library with us.'

I don't know why I was so weak. I turned to Luca and said, 'There's this thing I kind of have to do, so, em, yeah. I'll see you around.'

And Luca just shrugged like it didn't matter to him one way or another, and Conor said, 'Yeah, she'll see you around,' and Luca walked away.

I was raging with the two of them for bossing me around like that and with myself for letting them. And for the whole day I did the work I was supposed to do, but I did it loudly, banging things around until Veronica asked me, 'What on earth's got into you today, Allie?'

I texted Luca to say I was sorry for rushing off, and he said, 'Allie, it's grand. I understand you've other things to do. It's no problem. Stop saying sorry the whole time,' and I arranged to meet him at the playground again and I promised myself the next time Conor and Poppy bossed me about, I was going to stand up to them both.

I could tell the next day when I saw him swirling on his swing that Luca hadn't lost any sleep over it.

He smiled when he saw me.

'So you think it's the Hulk, then?'

For a second I hadn't a clue what he was talking about.

'It was just a guess,' I said, remembering.

'Pretty useless guess if you ask me. Allie, seriously. The Hulk? OK, sure, strong compared to a normal human and yeah, yeah, he might be able for Loki and everything, but the alternative – well, we're talking about a *lion* here. The king of the jungle. Muscles like rocks. Claws as sharp as meat hooks. Jaws thirty centimetres wide. Teeth like daggers. A lion would take on twenty Hulks, I reckon, and still be thirsty for more. Tear them limb from limb, he would.'

I stared at him for a while.

'I guess I hadn't really thought about that,' I said.

Luca stood up from the swing and started walking in the direction of the town, and I started following him.

'OK, then what about a Triceratops versus a T-Rex?'

'Luca, I haven't a clue. Why do you keep asking? And is this still the friendship test?'

'Ah, no. I was only joking about that. I just thought you might have a view,' he said.

'Well, I don't.'

'You should,' he said.

We'd reached the turn in the road.

'Would you condemn someone for asking the question, though? That's what I really want to know.'

'People can ask whatever questions they like. It's a free country,' I said.

'Exactly!' He laughed. It wasn't until we'd turned the next corner into Main Street that I realised where we were going.

CHAPTER 12

Spinellis' had come into being like the blossoming of a glamorous, unusual flower. Within just a couple of weeks, the toxic ghost of Jake that hung about his old shop had been swept and scrubbed away completely. You'd never think there'd been a fire in it, or that it used to be a horrible grimy shop where people only ever stood in queues, huddled and silent. Now it was full of a lovely, unexpected feeling and there was a dizzying buzz of freshly painted newness shining from every surface.

Luca showed me the customer area, all comfy and bright with round tables and strong chairs, and he showed me the main kitchen with its stainless-steel shine and a giant pale-blue fridge and the cooking equipment hanging from the ceilings and in the cupboards.

'This is amazing, Luca,' I said.

'You haven't seen the lights yet.' He told me to go outside again.

'Ready?' he said, before switching them on, and SPINELLIS' flashed out on to Main Street, throwing swirls of magic colour on the pavement in the middle of our jaded old town.

'Ah, yes,' Ariana said, startling me as she swooped out into the street, handing me a paintbrush the way you might give someone a bunch of flowers, 'the plan is coming to pass! When the venture is ready, the helpers arrive! Welcome, Allie Redmond! Welcome to Spinellis'. Come in. There is work to be done, but we are getting closer every day.'

I'd never painted anything in my life before. Ariana showed me to a smaller alcove off the main space. I pulled the brush across the white blankness of the wall, my first marks on Spinellis'.

We covered lots of ground and all the while music played and Luca, busy too and focused, chatted to me from time to time, making me feel like I belonged; and I was doing something properly useful for the Spinellis; and Ariana was dreamy and glad, humming to herself high up on the stepladder, working on the ceiling.

She made careful progress, and moved her own paint brush in graceful strokes like a dancer. When the ceiling was finished she climbed down to check it from a distance. And said she wanted to ask me something.

I told her she could ask me anything.

'Allie Redmond, I would like to offer you a job. I would like you to be the very first employee of Spinellis'.'

I wasn't able to answer at first.

'I'll let you and Luca discuss the proposition further, but I very much hope you will say yes. I have a feeling we will be lost without someone like you to help.'

She took off her apron and picked up her bag and told us she had some important business to take care of at the Clanfedden Inn.

'*Allora, miei amori*, see you both soon.' She floated by me and out the door. Her car with the hairdryer engine started up, and stuttered off.

Luca said, 'Hey, Allie, it would make everything a million times better if you came to work here, if you and I were a team.' And I thought about how I could make some difference after all. That I could be part of the history of a building that had once been a horrible business which robbed, and squeezed and starved people of their hope. That now it was going to be a good place, where people would be fed nice food, where they would feel connected, where they could be happy.

And for the first time in a long time, I stopped feeling worried. I stopped being afraid of Jake McCormack and uncertain about myself. I started to feel properly glad. I told Luca I'd love to work at Spinellis', of course I would.

He slipped behind the counter and started clinking about.

He carried over a fat teapot on a silver tray and placed it down between the two of us, pouring golden liquid into pale pink mugs. Steam floated in front of our faces. Gingermint tea doesn't taste like normal tea. It's much, much better. Hot, but cool too. And everything would have been perfect except that right then a horrible sound began to swell.

It was like the growl of a distant animal or the rumble of thunder. Luca and I looked at each other. The noise got closer and closer. There was the unmistakeable clatter and squeak and hiss of an enormous truck. It came grinding to a stop right in front of the Spinellis' bright new window, casting a dark shadow on both of us.

'Woah! Size of that thing!' said Luca, innocent and unaware.

Jake McCormack's shadow lurked in the driver's seat, all hunched up and huge-shouldered. His balaclava-covered face turned towards us.

I grabbed Luca by the arm, pulling him away from the window.

'Don't say anything. Don't look out. Wait till he's gone.'

Jake's truck stayed there for a good ten minutes or so.

I went on whispering to Luca, 'Keep pretending not to notice him. That's the safest thing to do.'

'It's McCormack, isn't it?'

'Yes,' I said, breathing fast and shivering a bit, 'it is. I knew this would happen. He mightn't have managed to burn you out of the place, but he hasn't given up.'

Then Jake's truck revved up again. Big, black pillows of smoke came belching out and he rumbled off.

'Oh, no,' I said when I'd been able to calm down a bit. 'This is really bad.'

'Is it?' asked Luca. 'Do you think there's something we should do?'

'It might be worth trying to get a message to him through Conor's dad. Apologising. Asking for his permission. Maybe if your mum did that, it would be a good idea.'

'Unlikely, I reckon,' Luca said, picking coloured paper clips from a small bowl on the reception desk and aiming them into a jam jar on the counter. 'In her whole life, my mother has never looked for permission to do anything. She always does the things she decides to do, not the things that other people tell her.'

And after that I didn't know what else to say.

I waited with Luca until Ariana got back. I wanted to be there when she found out about how Jake had been lurking outside, looking in, revving his engine.

'Well, there is no law against doing things like that, so if he wants to do it, we can't stop him.' Ariana had laughed her light-hearted laugh and I didn't understand how she could be like this, now that I was surer than ever that Jake was going to keep coming back and he would keep trying to intimidate them from high up in the seat of his truck. Goodness knows what else might happen. At the very least, customers might stay away, be afraid to come.

'Oh, you don't need to worry about any such thing,' Ariana reassured me. 'People need feeding in this town! Proper nourishment is absent. I can see it. I can feel it.'

Ariana said that there was longing and sadness in the souls of the people of this town. It was one of the reasons she was here.

The strongest clue that people needed help, she said, was not their air of down-troddenness or despair, for a less perceptive person might go about their business and see no evidence of this. What was remarkable about Clanfedden, she said, was the incongruous cheerfulness.

If anyone really took the trouble to look, they would see what she meant. It didn't take the skills of a mystic or a mind reader.

'People can be living desperate lives,' Ariana told me, 'inches from disaster, and never take off their masks. They reveal themselves in other ways, though. It's a kind of heroism. And when you can sense what they're really feeling inside, well, it's amazing really, the everyday bravery of simply surviving when inside you're falling apart, and outside your town has suffered terribly because of things beyond your control. It makes it all the more astounding that they can keep going, that they act as if they are happy.'

'What do you mean?'

'Oh, Allie, I've been to the Clanfedden Inn and it is there that I see it most. Goodness, the way people behave up there. Gulping down great buckets of alcohol, like it was a competition, not eating so much as a scrap of food before, or during, or after. Have you seen those great big glasses you need both hands to hold?'

'Pints?' I said.

And Ariana replied, 'One after the other! Fighting each other to buy the next round, lining up the drinks on the table like it's a challenge, singing songs, laughing and laughing until their faces are dangerously purple, as if they are about to have heart attacks, and there are tears . . . tears! Falling out of the eyes of men and everyone thinks it's happiness, they think it's joy.'

'Ariana, I'd be surprised if Clanfedden Inn hasn't always been like that. That's what people do in pubs.'

'Dearie me,' she said. 'Well, yes, you may be right. But this is different. This is an emergency. You know what it is, don't you?'

I shook my head.

'This town is living under a shadow,' she said. 'Nobody laughs like that, holding their stomachs as if they were going to get sick and choking with laughter as if they are going to die. It's not natural. No. That laughter. It's forced and it's guttural and it takes a great deal of courage. People only laugh like that when there's some terrible, deep secret in their midst. Some terrible threat.'

'Well, I hate to be the one to remind you,' I said, for I was still very worried, 'but there *is* a threat, Ariana, and the threat has a name. Jake McCormack.'

'Oh goodness, no. That's not who I'm talking about. I'm not afraid of that silly person,' she said.

CHAPTER 13

The refurbishment at Spinellis' kept happening fast. The opening was going ahead and that was that, and now I was going to be part of it.

Still, there was a lot more to be done before it was ready for its public. There were less than two weeks to go.

As well as the getting the restaurant looking nice, a huge clean-up was happening all over town and Ariana's team of builders were on the case again.

'Those flowers on the Clanfedden Bridge,' she said, 'they're the wrong kind. They will always bloom too fast and die too early. We can't have that any more.'

And she went down herself, to unhook each of the hanging baskets and give them the Ariana treatment, which meant lifting the old flowers out and putting new ones in.

'And,' she said another day, 'it will not do for those tennis courts, so close to us, to be in such an appalling state of filth and disrepair.'

I thought we needed to ask permission to get access to the courts, but Ariana said that was nonsense. It was clear that the courts had been abandoned. And in any case, it wasn't a matter of rights, she said; it was a matter of responsibility, of taking the initiative. Luca and I went along with her. She used a huge set of pliers to cut off the rusty padlock.

And though I was still a little worried, it turned out to be a lot of fun cutting the crazy overgrown grass with a bockety old lawnmower that Ariana had borrowed from Tina and Ciara Marshall. Getting rid of the rotting rubbish was a disgusting business. Ariana showed up with a plough and went in and churned up the earth of those old tennis courts that I couldn't ever remember anyone playing on. A silent man came with a great roller and he rolled out the ground flat and smooth.

The next day, a big package arrived for Ariana, and inside were crisp green nets with sturdy, white-stitched borders and when everything was in place the courts were beautiful, and the old fence was taken away and a new gleaming one was put in.

And Ariana bought twenty bright green balls and four wide rackets and put the balls in a big wicker basket and the rackets in an umbrella bucket. These would be kept in the restaurant and people would be able to have a game before a meal or after it, or even between courses if they felt like it.

And then it was the playground's turn. And soon instead of the broken slide and those grubby swings, there was now a gazebo, and fairy lights at night-time, and she cleared the little pond and planted quick-growing thick bushes around it and cleaned the rusty roundabout, installing on its central pole a spare pair of speakers so that music played when people got on. And during the day, people would be able to bring their children and get their coffee at Spinellis', and at night families would be able to take their teenagers to dinner.

'We know,' Ariana explained, 'that teenagers eat faster than their elders and cannot bear to sit in one place for too long, especially not with their parents.'

So now there would be things for them to do; they could walk down the lane to play tennis or turn to the right to the playground where they could swing dreamily on the sparkling new swing set, or dip their toes into the twinkling pond and this would be the perfect place for them to talk to each other about their dreams and desires the way teenagers should always be able to.

'The young must always have magical places, set apart,' she said.

Clanfedden felt brighter and better than it had for a long time, and it was nearly opening day and everything was almost ready.

Ariana had stocked the fruit shelves in the restaurant and a new sweet fresh smell had begun to fill the place. You could breathe it in. Raspberries, peaches, nectarines, lemons and limes, melons, apples, figs, bananas, avocados, apricots. Great blocks of black chocolate. Huge jars of cashews, hazelnuts, pine nuts, peanuts. All these lined up and ready for the following day when she planned to use this fresh sweet rainbow of fruit and nuts and delicacies to make her famous ice creams and pack the freezer with them. But it would be a shame not to have some of those plump fresh raspberries now. 'They are perfect,' she announced, sniffing them, selecting the fattest and plopping them into a big glass bowl. She squeezed in the juice of a shiny green lime and shook in some fine white sugar, on top of this sprinkling torn mint leaves that she'd plucked from the little herb greenhouse where twenty different plants had been set up under gently glowing lamps. Then she ground that fruity, sugary, zesty, herby mix together with the marble pestle that she kept in the pocket of her apron, finally glugging some of her home-made ginger ale on top. Mixing this a little more, she poured us each a glass. It was a liquid so richly pink that it almost hurt to look at it. We closed our eyes as we took the sips and Ariana laughed at my pleasure and amazement. We sat at the newly constructed counter, sipping that glorious drink, as she told us the rest of her plans:

'Opening night is now set! Two Thursdays from now. I have posters! We must start getting them up around the town.

'From then on, every Tuesday we'll give cookery lessons: we shall teach the people of Clanfedden the delightful secrets of home-made pasta; the pleasure of a properly made pizza base; the alchemy of sourdough bread; the joy of cakes; the simplicity of nutty meringues and the pure strategies of simple salads and sauces. Wednesday will be pizza night. Mondays will be *dolce* only: pastries, jellies, chocolate, panna cotta and cakes, all served with my special blends of fresh herbal teas. And on Friday and Saturday we will offer our very finest *à la carte* menu. Sunday we shall have to ourselves.'

She rose to her feet circling the room, smiling at the tables as if crowds of people were already there.

Something was bothering me. I couldn't stop thinking that there was another thing happening on Thursday week.

Whatever it was, the arrangements for the Spinelli opening were made now, and plans were firm, and I was committed no matter what. It would have been too late to change.

'But it will be our Thursdays which will be the most special of days. We will call it, *Aperto il Giovedì*! Open Thursday.

'On Thursdays, the prices will be only a suggestion! People will only pay what they can afford. That way, everyone will be able to come to Spinellis'. Nobody will be turned away.'

*

'No offence, but that's basically a terrible way to run a business,' Veronica said, when I tried to explain it to her on the phone. I'd remembered what had been bothering me about the opening of Spinellis'. It was happening on the same day as the book fair. I'd rung Veronica to explain. She was fine about it and I loved her for this. 'I do think you should drop in and explain the situation to Conor and Poppy. They'll be extremely disappointed, but I feel you must tell them face to face.' So I promised her that I would, just as soon as I had a moment.

I also told Veronica that Jake McCormack had been hanging around in his truck outside the restaurant and Veronica's voice sounded wise and worried: 'Oh dear. Well, I suppose it was only a matter of time. Maybe he was just curious. Let's hope he won't cause any trouble.'

He did cause trouble. With just a week to go he pulled up outside again, revving his engine, staring down in through the glass. Then after ten minutes or so he drove off again. I felt a pain in my chest and after he'd gone, I had to open the windows just so I could breathe. The day after that, when Luca and I were opening up with a whole load of important jobs planned, we found a note stuck on the door.

It said:

REMEMBER THIS PLACE IS NOT YOURS. YOU WILL HAVE NO LUCK IN CLANFEDDEN.

I wanted to call the police. But as usual, when we showed Ariana, she said the only possible response to something like that was to ignore it.

'As long as I have you as my two helpers,' she said, 'then all will be well. You and Luca do not need to worry about or be intimidated by the empty threats of someone who doesn't even show their face. You are only ever to think about the heart and purpose of Spinellis', and if you do that, and if this remains your focus, then everything is going to be fine.'

We sat back up at the counter then, and in the middle of this small, brave family, the fear of Jake McCormack seemed to loosen its grip on me.

'You have worked so hard,' I said. 'I really hope it's going to be OK.'

Luca and Ariana somehow made me feel that life was exciting and that there were adventures around the corner for me, adventures of a kind it had been almost impossible to imagine before.

Everything was different now. It was starting to show.

I didn't want to face Conor and Poppy, but Veronica said it was the right thing to do, so I called to the library. She said they were going to be very upset when I told them I was quitting the committee. She was right. They were.

'It's not my fault the book fair and the Spinelli opening

are on the same day,' I said to them. 'I can't be in both places at the same time. And I work for the Spinelli family now.'

'You were on the book fair committee before you even knew the Spinellis existed,' said Conor. 'And we know Luca is no good. I keep telling you. He got expelled and we don't even know for what.'

Poppy glared at me. 'They're dangerous. I don't know why you won't listen.'

'I won't listen because you're wrong,' I said. 'I'm surprised at you both. You haven't even given him a chance. You've just decided to believe the worst of him because it suits you to believe it. Luca is lovely. He's decent and he's good.'

'How do you know?' Poppy said, blowing bubble gum and snapping it menacingly near my face.

'I know because of the wide-openness of his face and because of the way he cares about his mother and because of how carefully he listens to me and because of how easy it is to talk to him.'

Poppy shook her head and Conor smiled pityingly.

'You're making a mistake,' he said. 'I hope you find out before it's too late. Luca Spinelli is no good.'

I hated that they had delivered their verdict and it felt like it was pretty much final and I hated that it meant Conor and Poppy were never going to be friends with Luca.

But I couldn't let it get to me, because there was something flickering inside me like a flame and the flame was because of Luca and nothing was going to put it out.

And yet, even though I had not wanted to listen to them, I couldn't stop thinking about the things Conor and Poppy had said – about how Luca must have done something pretty bad to get expelled and move town. And there were things about Luca; mysterious, silent kinds of things that did make me wonder what had happened before he came here, and what he might have done.

There was definitely some big secret and it definitely had to do with his past and perhaps it was something bad, on account of how he refused ever to talk about it. And there kept on being this one person who rang and rang and rang on Luca's phone, even though Luca never answered. And I wanted to know what those things were about and I wished he would tell me and I wished I knew why he would not.

CHAPTER 14

People even started calling in to the shop to wish Ariana and Luca the very best of luck, to tell them how brilliant the changes were what with the beautiful job they had done to the playground and the Bridge and the tennis courts. There were others, though, who were not so pleased. Conor's dad was worried that Jake might have an issue with how the town was changing without his permission. It wouldn't do for Jake McCormack to be any more furious than he already was. It wouldn't have been right if she didn't know what some people were saying, but Ariana just chuckled when I told her.

'Why would I need his permission?' she asked. 'Does Jake own the flowers? Does he own the tennis courts? Does he own the playground?'

'I don't know. Probably.'

'Well, if he does, then shame on him, and if he doesn't then no problem either!' she said. I tried to engage with this debatable logic but she shushed me. It was infuriating.

'Sometimes it's better to be free of the opinions of others, *mi amora*. There are times in your life when you just have to plough ahead and believe everything is going to turn out well.'

'Nod away at her,' Luca whispered. 'There's no point in arguing.'

'You see,' she continued, 'the very belief that all will be well contains a great kind of power. It's called, oh, how do you say it? *Una profezia che si autoavvera*.'

'A self-fulfilling prophecy,' interjected Luca again, and Ariana shouted,

'Yes! That's it! Exactly! A prophecy that realises itself! Now, please, I need you both to go into town and put up the last of our posters for the opening.'

Luca and I spread out. I took the top end of Main Street and he started at the bottom.

I was taping a Spinellis' poster on the noticeboard in the Mini Market when Conor and Poppy passed by on their skateboards.

'Allie, Allie, Allie,' said Conor, screeching to a stop.

'Hey,' I said, a little bit embarrassed, a little bit proud.

'What's the sign for?' asked Poppy, although I knew she already knew and if she didn't, she wouldn't have had to ask seeing as it was written all over the poster in huge clear letters.

'What's the story, Al?' Conor said. 'Seriously, tell us. Are you too good for us now that the Spinellis have basically adopted you? Now that you're working in their astoundingly fine eatery? Are you avoiding us? Funny how quickly you can drop your old friends, Al, as soon as someone shiny and new comes along.'

Part of me knew this was a bit true, but I didn't want to hear it. I tried not to feel ashamed of myself. But shame comes to the surface when the truth is told. Somehow they were strangers to me now. There was an iciness in Conor's voice too that somehow toughened me.

'You know what?' I said. 'The Spinellis are only trying to make things better in Clanfedden. I don't know what exactly is wrong with being involved with that.'

There was a silence.

'OK, I was just asking,' he said at last. 'We'd kind of like to see you, you know. We're not used to doing things without you.'

I watched them as they skated off. Poppy had on a new jacket and her nails were painted gold. She'd never have bought something new before without at least sending me a photo.

Thankfully, I didn't have time to dwell on stuff like that. There were flyers to be posted. There was an opening to get ready for.

*

There were plenty of moments when it hardly seemed possible we'd be ready, but when the night before the opening came, every single thing had been done. The walls were finished, white and pale eggshell-blue, and each of the chairs was a different shade of pink, and there were flowers and heavy wooden menus and a counter with a big, old-fashioned, golden cash register. It was like something from a fairy story, in the middle of Clanfedden. The loveliest thing of all was the alcove, a little bit apart from the rest of the space, separated by a fine silk curtain, pulled back with brass clasps. There were shelves of glass bottles and vases, some big and blue, some pale and purple, some dense and black. There were books on a shelf of their own. There was a picture in a silver frame of two girls, and there were wooden letters on the wall which spelled out RACHEL'S CORNER. The photo was of Ariana and my mother when they were young. Standing tall in tennis gear, staring determined and happy straight ahead.

'I hope you don't mind,' Ariana said quietly. 'I wanted her to be part of it somehow.'

And I hugged Ariana around her neck and said thank you. Thank you for remembering my mum, for having known her, for making her memory clear and not being afraid to put her name large upon the wall.

That night, to settle our nerves before the big day, we played tennis on the newly renovated courts and I thought about my mum and Ariana clapped at the sidelines and hung up flowers everywhere before heading back to the restaurant to make the finishing touches.

I beat Luca, but not by much. We were tired. We sat on the side, getting our breath back. I looked at him. Over the last few days, I'd found myself wanting to know his secrets more badly than ever.

'What happened in Dublin, Luca? I wish you'd tell me.'

He was quiet for just a moment, looking straight ahead. Then:

'Allie, I'm never going to talk about it. I'm not being smart; it's just that I don't want you to know, because you wouldn't like me any more and I really want you . . .'

'You really want me to what?'

'I really want you to like me. I've never wanted anything more in my life, to be honest.'

'I do like you, Luca.'

'OK, well in that case you should be able to tell me this . . .'

'What?'

'Panther versus dingo? Quick. First answer. Don't over think.'

'Definitely panther.'

'That was an easy one. How about chimp versus orangutan?'

'Orangutan!' I said, feeling like I was on a roll.

'Ah no, Allie, the orangutan is the gentleman of the jungle. The chimp's nothing but a hooligan in comparison.'

'OK, well, you live and learn,' I said.

A light, misty, invisible-curtain Clanfedden rain started to fall, the kind that makes your hair stick to your face and I decided I was going to try and forget about what might be in Luca's past. The floodlights threw three arches into the sky above our heads and Luca reached out and brushed a strand of hair from my cheek, and for a second it felt like we were floating.

I didn't get home until midnight and Dad was raging but I didn't even care.

I didn't feel like sleeping so I opened my window and I sat looking out for a bit, feeling the breeze, letting it cool my face. I thought about the things I already liked about Luca Spinelli. The way he smiled, the straight, honest way he spoke, the funny things he said.

'Please let Luca and his mum be OK here. Please let them keep liking it. Please help them make it work. Please make sure Jake McCormack stays away. Please let tomorrow be as great as it deserves to be.' I said it out loud. I don't know who I was asking. I guess it was a kind of prayer.

CHAPTER 15

'When you're cooking,' Luca said, 'it's vital to stay calm and happy. If you're stressed, it bleeds into the food, you see.'

I was like, 'Yeah, right,' and he was like, 'No, seriously.'

Luca sniffed each red fresh tomato before he sliced it open. He scooped the seeds out and put them aside. He showed me how to do the same, and to chop basil and to sprinkle salt and which huge pot we needed to use to make sure the sauce would cook in exactly the right way.

'Plan for many,' Ariana insisted, gliding around, lighting candles and humming a little tune. She lowered the lights and took out an old vinyl record and perched it on its roundabout machine. Luca and I put silver knives and forks on the tables just as Ariana had shown us and we folded a flock of coloured napkins, and we filled the water jugs with lemons and herbs, and we put flowers on the counter.

Ariana opened this book called the Spinelli family recipe book, which sat on a high slanted podium of its own with a special golden light shining down on it.

Luca polished the floor and wiped the counter and he plucked scalding glasses from the dishwasher, and shined them with a cloth, and held them to the light and it seemed as if a hundred tiny stars twinkled on his face.

And in the background from that spinning music box came beautiful voices of men, and I did not know what they were singing but it made my heart swell.

We looked around at the perfect shining restaurant. I saw Ariana's face in the soft light; I saw the work and the discipline. I was worried that no one would come. That maybe everyone would be too afraid to show their support. But people did come, and the first person to arrive was my dad and it looked as if he had put his rage and silence behind him for the night. I couldn't believe it.

'I understand there's astonishingly fine food to be had here,' he smiled, shaking Ariana's hand and then hugging her tight.

'Ah, Rory, how welcome you are, and how wonderful that you are here. *Fantastico!*'

'Dad, thanks a million for coming,' I said.

'Sure how could I miss it?' And I might have been imagining it, and I wasn't going to get my hopes up or anything, but there was definitely something of the old Dad in the way he said that to me.

With great elegance and sense of occasion, Ariana took my dad's coat and hung it on the hook alongside her pale, shell-pink jacket and showed him to Rachel's corner. Dad's chin quivered a little when he saw Mum's name on the wall and her picture in the frame and I thought he might be angry about that but he just nodded his head, and I went over and held his hand for a moment.

Soon some of Dad's friends from the pub were knocking timidly too and Ariana welcomed them all as warmly, showing them to their seats. Ciara and Tina arrived with cans of beer and the builders came, and so did Terry and Alice Morrison and Delilah Scully and practically every person from Clanfedden. They all kept saying how brilliant the place looked and what a wonderful job Ariana and Luca had done, how transformed it was, how before this, it had been a terrible place. Dirty and humid and full of the fever of greed and the sourness of loss.

The evening was beautiful and slow like a performance. Bread, baked that morning, had been cut into crusty soft strips and arranged on white plates with little bowls of deep green olive oil and blackest vinegar. And people kept on arriving until every table and chair was full. There was soup of oranges, carrots, spinach and garlic. My dad had two bowls of it, which made Ariana laugh. There was multi-coloured pasta with the freshest sauces, some tomato, some cream, and there were huge platters of gloriously colourful salads.

'Holy God but this is all lovely,' chuckled the Clanfedden people, munching away. And the crowd was big, and the place was noisy and full of laughter.

'I've never tasted anything like this food,' said Dad, whose eyes were glassy with delight. 'How on earth do you do it?'

'It's easy; it's all in there,' Ariana said, and she pointed at the Spinelli family recipe cookbook.

Ariana bustled around, smiling at everyone, not in the slightest bit amazed. She had been expecting them. She had known they would come. All along, she had been right.

Just as everyone thought they could eat nothing more, Ariana brought cheeses out on grey, slate boards with crisp baked crackers and after that, the tiniest ornamental dessert morsels as small as jelly tots made with ganaches and glazes and dots of custard and miniature candies, and honest to goodness if you could die from the pleasure of beautiful food, the whole lot of us would all be dead now.

As the happy evening came close to its end, Ariana stood and tapped her wine glass.

'I am going to make a speech,' she said.

She talked about the wonderful welcome she and Luca had been given by the people of Clanfedden, and how lucky she felt.

And in that newly-occupied, freshly-painted place, a warm feeling encircled us all. New things were going to be possible in Clanfedden, we thought; it could be full of eventfulness and togetherness. And people might be happier and less timid and less downtrodden, and it was all because of the Spinellis.

It seemed that tiny sparkles shot from the wine glasses and little shiny fizz-dots flung out from the silver spoons and forks and knives. The Spinellis had done it. They had turned Jake McCormack's place of poison into this venture, full of pride and promise.

My dad lit up too; telling stories that turned out to be so interesting that we forgot how late it had become, and Ariana poured out a lemony drink of golden liquid, which glowed in the candlelight. Dad tipped it into his mouth. He frowned as if he was thinking hard, and then announced: 'Citrusy ambrosia!' and Ariana laughed.

'Never,' she said, 'has Limoncello been described so perfectly.'

Luca and I drank sparkling water with elderflower cordial that Ariana had made from blossoms she'd gathered from a shrub called *elderflower*. She said they grew everywhere in the fields around Clanfedden. It was aromatic and herby, and it tasted like magic too.

'You found it in the fields?' I asked, not believing that anything growing around here could taste like this.

'There are treasures everywhere, if you care to look,' she smiled at me and raised a glass.

I suddenly wished there had been no clash and that

Conor and Poppy and Veronica had been able to come. They seemed the only people in the town who were not here, and just for a second, I wondered how they were getting on. I worried the fair would be deserted considering how so many people had come. It gave me a pain in my stomach, just for a second or two, when I thought about that.

After the last scrap had been eaten, the summer night grew a little colder. Ariana lit the stove and we all sat with cups of gingermint tea, and there was that comfortable silence that sometimes settles around people who have eaten well together, and who can sit wrapped in a blanket of silky flavours without needing to fill up the space with talk. Only the crackle of the logs and the whisper of the flame.

Eventually everyone left, calling their thanks behind them, and their promises to return. There were still mountains of food.

'Will we throw this away?' I asked, and Ariana held her finger in the air and her giant blue-stoned ring flashed triumphant.

'Throw it away? Why, never, my darling girl! I grew up in a place where food was precious and money was scarce and in a place like that you learn many skills; among them, a talent for preservation: pickling, salting, smoking, sugaring, drying, fermenting, packing, canning. Nothing will ever get wasted at Spinellis'!

'This will be one of the secrets of our success. Properly done, it's like locking away treasure during the sunshine, so you can take it out in dark winter when things seem at their worst, their most desolate, their least fruitful. And when the time comes and you peel open the lid, light comes out, and again, you can taste the glory.'

'Do you reckon everyone here thinks she's a weirdo?' Luca whispered to me.

'Clanfedden is full of weirdos,' I replied. 'By my calculations, she should be fitting right in.'

Later, Poppy texted to tell me no one had showed up for the book fair. Not a single person. After all their preparation and all their planning and all their work. They waited two hours for the crowd that never came. All the musicians and poets went home early.

Poppy said Veronica had been furious, but I knew that wasn't true, because Veronica never got angry about anything; and besides, Veronica understood me, and she was always on my side.

CHAPTER 16

Open Thursdays became famous in Clanfedden.

The Spinellis taught me many things: how to peel aubergines and cut them into the thinnest lengthways slices; the slow, careful way that tomatoes need to be stewed; the neat, clipped way you have to pick a leaf of basil from its plant; and the curling caress you need to learn if you are to achieve exactly the right fineness in the shavings from the huge, bumpy block of parmesan that sat in the coldest part of the kitchen in a space of its own, on a slab of black marble, like some ancient knobbled trophy.

Melanzane parmagiana. Because it was my favourite, it became the Spinelli special.

Spinellis' was more successful than anyone could ever have predicted. Soon the word had spread beyond Clanfedden and people came from other towns and then the news spread further again, across the whole country and there were articles in newspapers and photographs in glossy magazines and I could hardly believe how the world had begun to talk about our town.

I loved Ariana, I realised. And Luca Spinelli. If I'm honest, I didn't just grow to like him. To be accurate, it hadn't taken that long for him to become the most cherished, the most beloved of the friends I'd ever had.

At Spinellis', there were certain and specific ways of doing things, called *modi di fare le cose,* and there were many of them. The way food should look on a plate, the way certain utensils should be taken out, how they should be cleaned and how they should be put away again, the importance of leaving plenty of time between courses, what kinds of drinks go with which type of food, double-washing the organic lettuce (on account of caterpillars sometimes hiding in the green folds), how to chop and how to fry and how to peel and how to press.

There was a special way to clean pulp from the juicer and a particular angle you needed to hold the glasses up to the light to make sure they were completely clean and clear.

There were rules of politeness too:

Always take a customer's coat.

Meals don't begin until everyone is sitting.

Be prepared to help with the menu, but never choose on anyone's behalf.

Don't make people feel hurried or unimportant or difficult.

Act as if the customer's every wish is what you have been put on the earth to provide, unless their wish happens to be outlandish or vexatious, in which case, simply ignore it.

Be alert.

Keep it simple.

It confused me that a lot of the time the sacred Spinelli family recipe book wasn't even consulted.

'Oh, it's like musicians in an orchestra,' Luca explained when I asked him why not. 'You don't have to look directly at the conductor. You just need to know the conductor is there.'

And I grew to love that magnificent idea; that food is like a symphony and we were the orchestra, and an old recipe book was our silent conductor.

From the very start, the crowds kept coming, and Ariana came into her own. She made huge jars of peanut butter from scratch, and fresh bread every day. Even by 11 p.m. the slices were still fingerprint soft. Free sandwiches was another one of the many perks of working at Spinellis'.

'Never go home hungry,' she'd say to me. 'I can't have your father thinking you're being exploited. We must take good care of you.'

Ariana's night-time sandwiches were like nothing I'd tasted anywhere. Using their own freshest bread and the olive oil sent and delivered from her cousin's farm in Poggibonsi, and filling the sandwiches with careful combinations, those sandwiches weren't just food. They were works of art. They were soothers of the soul. She showed me how to make them and soon you couldn't tell the difference between hers and mine. And each night I would go home feeling strengthened and capable because of skills I had learned, and because of how the Spinellis were making such a big and brilliant difference in this town.

But I have learned that perfect happiness is an impossible thing.

Jake had not gone away, and soon he started driving past again, in his menacing truck. I tried not to let it frighten me. But whenever I heard him coming, a shiver rolled through me like a cold wind, and a silent shadow fell.

I hated the way the mention of his name could freeze the blood inside my veins, and how the great shadow of his juddering truck could squeeze the light and sparkle out of the place and turn silver to pewter and extinguish the gold of the Spinelli air.

When he lurked there, a few people would look nervously at Ariana, who would never break her stride. And a silence would suddenly replace the happy murmur and a tension would fill the place with edgy echoes. And then Jake would rev the engine and screech off into the night.

'What on earth is that Jake McCormack up to?' someone asked one evening, and Ariana said:

'Oh, honestly, do not give it another moment of thought. It's simply bluster. That note, those silly threats. What has he actually done?'

'He tried to burn your place to the ground,' I reminded her, but everyone hushed me then, saying again there was no evidence of that.

'Listen,' Ariana continued. 'I know of men like Jake. They are made of nothing but empty threats. That fellow relies on his reputation rather too much, I would say.'

I felt guilty about Veronica and the book fair, so as soon as the excitement settled a bit, I called in to tell her all the news, and to say hi.

'Hello, stranger,' she said. 'Fancy seeing you here. What's up?'

'Oh, nothing. I suppose I miss the library a bit, but Conor and Poppy are practically not even talking to me any more so I'm thinking there's not much point in coming anyway.' I looked up at her. 'You weren't angry about me not coming to the fair?'

'Angry, me?'

'Conor and Poppy said you were furious.'

Veronica laughed. 'Sometimes people attribute fury to other people when they're feeling it themselves,' she said. 'Things change and that's OK,' she went on. 'You are very busy now, with the new place and with Luca Spinelli and his mother, and I am so glad for you. Just remember my dear, I am still your refuge. Still here if you ever need me.'

'Veronica, I wish you'd come to the restaurant,' I blurted. 'It would be a chance to see Ariana, and I know that if you got to know Luca, you'd really like him.'

'What makes you think I don't like him already?' she smiled.

'I don't know, but Conor and Poppy have all these things against him and he's so much nicer than they are prepared to admit and so is Ariana, and I'm not one bit surprised any more that Mum and she were such friends.'

'Aren't you?' said Veronica.

'No, and their business is just so great, and their food is delicious and honestly, Veronica, working at the Spinelli restaurant has made me so very happy.'

Veronica listened and nodded and waited for me to finish, and then she said, 'Look, just be cautious, Allie. Sometimes things are not as they seem to be. Try not to be so hard on Conor and Poppy. You've known Poppy your entire life. And Conor has been a good friend to you for a long time now too. You don't really know the Spinellis, however much you think you do. You only know what they've told you themselves. Glitter is not always golden. Remember that. It pays to hold on to your friends.'

I told her about Jake's menacing behaviour outside the restaurant and how Ariana kept saying there was nothing to worry about.

Her face went tight. 'Ariana is very gravely mistaken,' she said. 'Jake McCormack's threats are never empty. You know this, and so do I. You're right to be concerned.'

I nodded.

'Whatever happens, this library will always be your refuge and your safety and your shelter from the storms. It is here if you need it.'

It was great to talk to her. I couldn't stick around, though. My shift at Spinellis' started in fifteen minutes and I couldn't be late.

That had been another record night. Our faces were sweaty from the work, and Ariana was serving the digestifs out front. You don't have a second on nights like that. Your brain never stops.

We bumped into each other, Luca coming out from the back kitchen and me on the way in. It wasn't a little bump; it was a huge bash, both of us moving at speed.

'Oh no, sorry, oh Allie,' he said, and I realised my nose was bleeding. He got out the first aid kit and held a pad of cotton wool up against my nose, tilting my head back.

'I think you'll live,' he said at last. 'But I feel terrible for clobbering you like that.'

He kept his hand against my nose and then he put the other one flat on my cheek and I didn't even care about the bleeding or the soreness because it was like there was something fizzing inside me. And even though the noise of the crowd was huge, and there was much to be done, he was looking at me and I was looking at him. And that was it. I felt a feeling that I'd never felt before. A feeling that doesn't have a name.

'Allie,' he whispered and leaned very close up to me and I could feel the warmth of his body and I could hear the breath in my lungs and the heart in my chest and the blood in my veins.

'Yes. Yes, Luca.'

'There's this thing I've been meaning to ask you, and I think this is the time.'

'What?'

'Do you think . . . I mean, would you be able to . . .'

'Luca, come on, tell me.'

'Could you possibly say whether . . .'

'It's fine, Luca, seriously. You can ask me anything.'

'OK then.' He breathed very deeply, and I think I did too. 'Would a scorpion kill a tarantula?'

I grabbed the tea towel from my waist and started whacking him on the arm, kind of gently, and he was laughing and so was I, and a decision landed on me in a way decisions very rarely ever do, and I pulled him closer and he put his hand on my waist and I put my hand on his and then in the back room to the tune of the clink and clash and swell of laughter from the customers in the front, Luca gave me a kiss and I gave him one back and it felt like the whole world had become suddenly secret, suddenly soft, suddenly thrilling.

But I cannot bear to think about this now, considering how it seems so long ago, even though it is not, and considering what a lovely thing it was, and considering what terrible things have happened since.

CHAPTER 17

Conor: 'Look, I know you're going to think this is jealousy or something, but I promise you it's not.'
Allie: 'What are you talking about?'
Conor: 'I've heard more about the rumours. He had something to do with a violent incident. He's done some horrible damage. He'll do the same here.'
Allie: 'I know him much better than you do. None of the stories are true.'

Obviously, I didn't mention to Conor that I had kissed Luca and that every time I saw him now, I wasn't able to breathe properly.

'Imagine there was a lion in the pantry, would you say it would be stupid to go out there?'

'Very,' I said.

'What if I brought one of these?'

Luca picked up one of the restaurant chairs and began lunging.

'Would I have at least a fighting chance then, do you think?'

'Doubt it.'

'What do you reckon I could throw to distract him?' he asked.

'Peanut butter or cheese?'

'Don't be an idiot,' he said, dodging, sidestepping. 'Lions have no interest in nut or dairy products. Raw meat. That's the only thing they're interested in.'

'I'm not talking about lions. I'm talking about your sandwich, what do you want in it? And put down that chair. You'll break something.'

'So what about the Hulk and a lion?'

'Luca, you've asked me that before and I've no idea why you keep on about it. I haven't a clue.'

'Why not?'

'Because I never think about things like that.'

'You should,' he said, trying now to balance on one leg, still holding the chair high. 'You should think it through very carefully. You should always know the answers to those kinds of puzzles. It's important.'

'It's not important. It's not even slightly relevant.'

'Not relevant? Allie Redmond, what are you saying? It's

crucial to everything – knowing who can outsmart you, who can outrun you, when to stand and fight, when to run away, who's your friend, who's your enemy. Those things matter. You never know when information like that could suddenly become critical. A crisis can hit, and you won't have time to figure it out on the spot. In any case, if there was a lion in the pantry, and you did have to face him, you'd only be scared for the first part of the fight.'

'Eh, no. I reckon I'd be scared pretty much all the way through. And before it. And after.'

He put the chair down and stood on it hitting the air with his fist in fake triumph, then bowing as if to a large audience.

'Luca, how come you're so weird?' I said, not really meaning it.

'Can't help it. It's in the blood,' he replied cheerfully. 'Root of all my problems, I reckon.'

'Who were your friends before you came here?'

He sat on the chair then. 'I really would prefer not to say,' he replied, and there was that flicker at the side of his face, that tiny pulse.

I looked around at the jars of herbed tomatoes and the pots of pickled vegetables and the barrels of flour and sugar and the huge cylinders full of pasta and the pots with wooden spoons sticking out of them.

'Seriously, though, are you ever going to tell me what you and your mother are actually doing here?'

He was up on the counter by then, swinging his legs, munching a handful of hazelnuts.

'It's not just the restaurant, is it?'

'Allie, I really, really don't want to talk about it.'

'Don't you think it would feel good to tell someone? Someone you can trust. Someone who's not going to judge you. Someone like me.'

'I just can't,' he said. 'I don't have the courage.'

I wish I could say that what I did next was because of my love for him, or how it was because I cared about him, or other good, noble reasons, but the truth is, it was curiosity that made me do it.

Ariana had sent me back to the store room to get some more coffee beans, and there was Luca's phone, just lying there on a high stool and at the very moment I noticed it was there, it started to ring.

It was the same number that he was forever ignoring and never answering.

I just wanted to find out. That's all.

So that is how I ended up speaking to Tom Cranfield.

'Luca, Luca, I've been trying to get a hold of you for weeks!' Tom Cranfield's voice sounded friendly, almost musical. Not the kind of voice you'd spend a whole summer trying to avoid.

'It's not Luca,' I said. 'It's a friend of his.'

'Oh.'

I asked him what his name was, and he told me.

'How is he?' was the next thing he said.

I told him that things were going really well for Luca in Clanfedden.

'Did he really leave the school because of something that happened on a trip?' I heard myself asking then.

'Yes, a terrible thing. We—'

The door burst open and Luca came in.

'Allie, we need the coffee . . .'

I had thrown his phone back on the stool, but it was too late. He'd seen.

'Eh, Allie, what's going on here? What were you doing with my phone?'

'Nothing,' I lied.

He grabbed it.

'Hello,' Luca said.

'Luca, it's Tom, please let me talk to you,' shouted Tom, so loud that I could hear too.

'You've been on my phone? Talking to Tom Cranfield?' Luca stared at me, pale-faced.

'Luca, look, it was ringing. I answered by accident. I just wanted . . .'

'Luca, Luca,' shouted Tom.

'YOU'VE been having a talk with HIM on MY phone?' he said. 'What the hell?' He hung up then and stood looking at me, and something in Luca's eyes changed then like they had gone a shade darker and it was like a horrible, angry swollen cloud seemed to float across the room. Luca stood in front of me.

'What did he say to you?'

'I asked him about why you left.'

It felt important to be honest now, since I'd done such a devious thing.

The Clanfedden rage had spread.

'Listen, Luca, I'm sorry, but let's not fight about this. Our friendship's too important,'

The sparkle in Luca's eyes had gone out. A deadness had landed on him. When he spoke next, he sounded like a different person.

'I didn't ask to be your friend. My mother needed some help in the restaurant, that's what it was. She thought it would be good for you. She felt bad for you.'

It hit me like a punch.

His eyes were cold. 'Allie, right, since you just won't leave it alone, stay here. I'm going to explain the whole bloody thing to you, OK?'

'OK,' I said.

'But after it we're not going to be able to be friends. It's a pity. But it's gone too far now. So here's the story. Here goes.'

A noise like a great explosion shuddered in the air. Another fire, I thought, turning from him and running through the doors.

From the back kitchen, we hadn't heard the rumbling of his truck or seen the darkness of shadow approaching.

The customers were all staring, forks poised. The big window of the Spinelli shopfront was smashed. Ariana was standing unmoving, her expression disbelieving. Glass kept on falling to the ground like a waterfall of frozen drops and the pieces skittered and bounced like hailstones and the huge masked figure of Jake McCormack stood at the window looking at us.

Everyone stayed completely still as he marched over to the podium and grabbed the Spinelli family recipe book.

'Do not cross me,' he growled, as everyone stared. His voice was low and the threat in it made me shiver. 'Never muscle in on Jake McCormack's turf. Nothing good will come of that. All of you, take heed.'

He climbed back up into his truck and drove away.

Everyone looked still like a picture. 'Everybody,' Ariana addressed the customers, 'don't you see? There is no need to be frightened. I have no fear of a bully who will not show his face. He's the coward. We can be brave. All we need to do is to stand up to him.'

'She's right,' said Luca, though I'm not sure who he was talking to but he'd grabbed her car keys.

'Luca, where are you going?' I asked.

He told me he was going after Jake. 'If I circle round the back way, I might be able to catch him on the bridge,' he said with a new, grim edge in his voice. And I kept begging him not to. And Ariana, who had never been afraid of Jake, was now afraid for Luca because of the look in his eyes and the greyness of his face and the things he might do. And she called him her love in Italian, and he told her not to call him that.

'Please don't do this,' I said. 'You've nothing to prove to anyone.'

'I have plenty to prove. You are wrong. Get out of my way.'

I ran after him. 'Stop this, Luca, what are you thinking?' But he pushed me and ran straight through the broken window and over to the car faster than anyone could have followed him, and I saw him start it up and head off up the back road to try to catch up with Jake McCormack.

PART 4

ON THE BRIDGE

LUCA SPINELLI

CHAPTER 18

There was a horrible truth behind why I left Dublin and now Allie knew it. She knew because she had talked to Tom Cranfield, who can only have told her that I had been a loser. The victim of taunts and bullying. The target of everyone's malice in Ashfield.

A group of people in my class had it in for me for as long as I could remember. Every day, they would recite a list of everything that was wrong with me, their own noxious pledge of allegiance to the degradation of my dignity. They chanted my pathetic failings, sometimes following me around while they did it:

'Luca, ooh Luca, where did you get your hair cut?'

'Luca, where did you buy your shoes?'

'Luca, is that your face or did your neck throw up?'

I felt ugly because of the things that they said, and my

hair was always bad, no matter what I did to it, and my shoes were terrible.

My mother was prepared to get me the right clothes, or the proper haircut, or whatever it took – that wasn't the problem. The problem was that soon as I got the right shoes, they were immediately going to become the wrong ones.

It was as if there was a secret code that everyone except me had access to and a password to acceptance that changed on a daily basis according to patterns and rules that I would never know.

Slowly, I had started to believe the things that Tom Cranfield and his friends said to me. That I was stupid and pathetic and I looked terrible and I was basically no good. Everything I did was an aggravating signal to them; I ate the wrong food and I said the wrong things and I wore the wrong clothes and I carried the wrong bag and I owned the wrong phone, and I had the wrong hair.

At the heart of it, there is a mystery about how a person's name is made or broken, and I honestly can't remember how it started. I don't think anyone can. It hardly matters anyway. The groundwork had been done. The foundation stone of my wretchedness had been a long time in the laying. A lot of people had a hand in it. But I think, looking back, it was the thing I said to Tom in school one day that marked the beginning of the end.

*

It was the start of a new school year after the holidays and Mr Quirke, for reasons best known to himself, had put Tom and me sitting next to each other. I don't know why I said what I did, why it came popping into my head and then out of my mouth, but I think it had something to do with Tom's glaring, judgemental silence. Silence like that can make a person nervous. And those were in the days when I still had hope that Tom Cranfield was not a complete tosser.

I was naïve, of course, but I thought it might have only been a matter of making a positive connection. I thought maybe there was a key to finding his better side – like, if I made moves to start an interesting conversation perhaps the nasty shell that surrounded him might melt away, and I might find a decent person underneath. Like I say, naïve.

'Tom, hey Tom, hello.'

He glanced at me – a lazy, casual moment.

'Question for ya.'

'What?' he said and I coughed a little and paused for focus.

'Who'd win a fight to the death between a lion and the Hulk?'

That is the question I asked. That is what I said.

Tom swivelled his chair around to stare at me more carefully in a menacing way that I would come to know well. He repeated my question word for word, in a high and squeaky voice.

'If you're trying to imitate me, it's not very good,' I said, even though it was too late to stand up for myself.

After that, the mocking and sneering became so relentless that even the mood-blind Mr Quirke picked up on it.

Mr Quirke was apparently an expert on my mental state. He told me how I seemed 'to be quite isolated', as if I didn't already know that, and that I 'didn't tend to reach out to my peers', and that for some reason, I seemed 'to pitch ideas and conversations that the other classmates didn't quite identify with'.

He must have meant the stupid question I asked Tom out of the blue. It was my nerves that made me do it. There was no one else to blame. The whole thing was my fault.

Mr Quirke came up with a litany of contradictory and useless advice.

'You should not try too hard, socially, I mean. You just need to be yourself, let people come to you,' he said.

'And don't go around asking questions about Hulks and lions any more. I mean, come on, Luca, that's asking for trouble. At your age, it's not the kind of thing that's of interest to anyone.

'Perhaps you might make more of an effort?' he'd suggested finally. 'And keep your head down.'

He spoke in that happy, certain tone that fills up the

voices of adults who think that there are no impossibilities or logical conflicts in the instructions they give, and that anyone's problems can simply be solved just by following their advice.

I couldn't be bothered trying to explain.

Tom was an idiot. I knew it, and probably everyone else in the class knew it too, which goes to prove that even an idiot can become powerful and get away with terrible things.

I personally think how someone reacts to hypothetical questions about whether the Hulk would beat a lion is a good way of understanding the difference between decent human beings and idiots. I mean, they don't have to be *right*. They just have to try.

Decent people let you ask whatever questions you feel like asking and they consider the questions seriously. That's what decent human beings do to each other.

My mother tried to help too. She went on about how reputations at school are not real.

'It doesn't matter what people think of you at school. If they really knew you, they'd all be clamouring to be your friend.'

And I know she wanted to make me feel better and I didn't have the heart to tell her the truth, which is that when your class has created a target and when that target is you, there is nothing to be done except whatever it takes to try to make it intact to the end of each day. In the moment-to-moment, survival-focused world of the underdog, there's no time for anything else.

From the start I begged my mother not to talk to anyone about the school situation. I was going to be fine, I tried to persuade her, and even if I wasn't, there was nothing she was going to be able to do to make things better, no matter how powerful she felt, regardless of how resilient she was.

I wished I hadn't said a word to her about the situation, but now that I had, I tried to make her understand the difference between her world and mine. When I found out she'd already made an appointment, that's when I began to panic. I had to make sure that my mother wouldn't come into school, speaking Italian, doing her best but making everything worse.

'Mum, the whole thing is sorted out already,' I'd lied to her in desperation. 'Myself and Tom Cranfield are the best of friends now.' And she marvelled at how quickly this had been resolved and I was relieved that she'd believed me so fully and so happily.

When the school trip to France was announced my mother said the timing couldn't have been better for myself and Tom to get some good quality time together now that we were such good friends.

And you could see so much pure hope shining out of her that, for a little while, I almost began to believe that myself.

CHAPTER 19

As it turned out, at the fun fair in Paris, Tom had smiled at me and talked to me a lot. It was totally out of character. It made me think we really were becoming friends.

I even trusted him enough to tell him about my mortal fear of heights and he nodded, like he was listening, like he cared.

A game, he said, let's play a game. Everyone had to put on a blindfold and go on an attraction. When it was my turn, I made Tom and his cronies promise they weren't going to make me go on to something high up and they said, 'Of course we won't do that. What do you take us for?' They told me not to be a killjoy. Put on the blindfold, they said. Play the game. Don't be a spoilsport. Trust us. It's going to be fun.'

The rollercoaster had locked down and was starting to move by the time they took the blindfold off and, when I realised what was happening, and where I was, I fainted. Someone tried to throw water on me, but they missed my face, and got water on my trousers. When I regained consciousness, they all told me I'd peed my pants, which for the record, I had not.

Maybe it doesn't sound that bad now, to some people. But I won't ever forget:

How almost all of my classmates were involved and how most stood smirking on the sidelines while I begged and I begged to be allowed off. Not one person in my class had tried to stop what was happening, even though they had all known what the plan was. How fast and terrifying the ride had been. How terrible my screams were, even to my own ears.

Someone had recorded the whole thing on their phone. By the weekend the link had been sent to me and I'd watched it. I had seen this awful moment at the end when the ride has stopped and when I am climbing out of the seat. The camera zooms in on my crotch, where there is a big, dark, wet patch, and there is that stupid laughter that you only ever hear in schoolyards or on school trips – hysterical, cruel.

And then the camera pulls back, and I look into it and you can see that I am lost and that my spirit has been destroyed and I am crying. And I would never be able to forget how I was that boy.

Anyone who saw that video would also know of the

sounds that had surrounded me that day, captured in the recording, sounds of malicious delight which is one of human nature's worst and strangest and most mystifying emotions.

It would have been weak and pathetic to ignore what had happened. Everyone knows that you only have a small window of opportunity to set things straight after something like that.

I was going to be strong.

That night in the hostel, I went to Tom's room, planning to make a stand, even if the consequences were going to be terrible. I was going to fight him, take back my dignity from him and his friends. I threw a single punch and missed him and fell over.

Their retaliation was vicious and accurate, and I found that I could not fight back. I was too broken. They'd taken my strength and my spirit away.

Somebody ran down the corridor to wake Mr Quirke up. Mr Quirke came running down the hostel corridor, wearing only a pair of Y-fronts, an image that can only have added to the post-traumatic distress that was to follow.

Mr Quirke gave me a quick examination during which he held me by my shoulders and peered at me through his glasses, and he decided I didn't actually look that bad and he went on about how this had been the sort of thing that sometimes happens 'on tour' and he didn't intend to make 'too big a thing' of it.

But the next day my face was swollen and blackened, and one of my eyes was almost completely shut. Going to a doctor in France would have meant everyone would have missed the flight home so Mr Quirke made the decision to notify my mother, and then simply press on to get me home with the rest of them, and to hope for the best.

The plane trip was hushed, and I was separated from everyone else, up at the front in a window seat with my face turned to the clouds.

Throughout the flight I couldn't read or listen to music or anything. I kept looking at my blossoming black eye in the reflection of the little oval window. I sort of liked the way it looked, to be honest, which was a wrong thing to feel, I am sure.

The doctor and my mother were at the airport when we landed. A single tear slid down my mother's face when she saw me, and, after one long hug, she held her arms unnaturally straight by her side. I looked down. For a while all I could look at were my mother's hands, the marbled furrows between her whitening knuckles.

We were taken into a side room normally used for smugglers, I reckoned. I was too embarrassed to speak.

The doctor tipped the rim of a bottle on to a small cloud of cotton wool and cleaned my face, which stung, and he put little white strips across a cut I didn't know I had, and he made a joke that no one laughed at, about being in the wars. Mr Quirke offered to drive us home but Mum said no. Her voice was steady and low and it sort of scared me.

'We are all right, Mr Quirke, thank you. I will take my Luca home.'

I wished she hadn't called me *her Luca*. It didn't do anything to help the situation.

In the car, I sat in the back as usual and Mum kept turning around to look at me, saying things like, 'Oh, Luca.'

And I kind of wanted to comfort her and reassure her that everything was fine, and this was all a huge drama about nothing, but I guess that wasn't true. I didn't want to have to talk about it. I wanted to go to my room and lie on my bed and look at my ceiling and not think about anything.

My mother was going to the school for a focused discussion. I pleaded with her not to. I told her she was probably going to make things worse, but she said that this time she must act.

'Mum,' I said. 'I can put up with the fact that it happened. I can get over the things that they did. If you're going to do anything then do something about the video.' She nodded and said she would do everything in her power. I didn't know if everything in her power would be enough.

I lay on my bed while she was gone, earphones in, music loud. When she came back from her school meeting, she tapped on the door and asked if she could have a chat.

'We have a strategy for dealing with the video,' she said. 'There is legislation now called "the right to be forgotten". We are going to activate it. Mr Quirke is fully supportive. And, as well as that, we have agreed that the ringleader must pay a price.'

'What?' I propped myself up on my elbows.

'They are going to suspend Tom Cranfield. Mr Quirke himself says it is the least that should be done.'

Things were not going to end well. But explaining this to my mother or to Mr Quirke would be like speaking to them in a language that neither of them understood. So I flopped back down on my bed, turning over on to my stomach.

'Thanks, thanks a million, that's great, Mum, thanks for letting me know. Now, no offence or anything, but I'm feeling kind of tired. I'd like to be on my own.'

For three weeks after that, I kept going to school and no one kept on talking to me. The video was still in circulation. I knew it because I checked YouTube every night and every night the record of my humiliation was still there.

Tom had been suspended, so he didn't have a chance to apologise even if he'd wanted to, which I was sure he did not. I saw him one day sitting in the back of his father's car while his two sisters got dropped off, the girls hopping out, skipping in glittery shoes across the yard, bright pink bags rattling and jangling on their backs.

The window was open. It was my chance and I took it.

'I've lost all my fear, you know,' is what I said, because it felt true at the time. 'You can do no more to me.'

He looked at me for a second with no readable expression, and then he turned his face away.

My mother had taken to coming into my bedroom every evening by then, to say goodnight to me, and I'd taken to lying with my face in the pillow. I always sensed her approaching warmth, but I put my hands up around my head so in the end all she was able to kiss were my fingers. And she would sometimes whisper something about how this whole situation would pass and how everything was going to be OK and again how proud of me she was.

By the time we were ready to leave for Clanfedden, the video was gone. You couldn't find anything about it or about me anywhere on the internet. My mother and Mr Quirke had kept going until they'd got a result, and it was only a small mercy by then, but still I was grateful for it.

In the middle of the goodbye party that our neighbours had organised, Mr Quirke rang. He wanted me to rethink. 'It would be quite wrong,' he said, 'for the perpetrator to be coming back to school and for you not to be.' He asked, now that everything had been erased, might I consider changing my mind. But just because something has been erased doesn't mean it is gone. Anyway, I said, I didn't have any say in the matter. It was too late. Everything was arranged. My mother's mind was made up and we were committed.

'Oh, well, look, I just want to say the very best of luck, Luca. And remember, you should be proud of yourself for getting to the other side of this. You have survived it – and you should try to remember that if ever your spirit is flagging. What doesn't kill you makes you stronger, isn't that what they say?'

I thanked Mr Quirke. I knew he was just trying to be nice. I didn't tell him that this was the stupidest saying I'd ever heard in my life. What doesn't kill you can still make you weaker. What doesn't kill you can lessen and belittle you. What doesn't kill you can drive you insane.

CHAPTER 20

I didn't know what made Tom Cranfield suddenly want to get in touch. He'd ignored me completely in Dublin. It wasn't until I got to Clanfedden that his calls had started.

I thought I could move on. I thought I could leave it behind. I thought the best way was to have no contact with anyone from Ashfield, especially not him. And for a while that seemed to work. Everything was going fine in Clanfedden and we had the restaurant, and I met Allie and I was properly happy.

I should have known that things like that don't go away, that you can't rub them out. I should have known the night was coming, the night it all came back.

Seeing Allie on the phone, realising she was talking to Tom, I knew then that none of it had faded at all – that it was still there, clear and crushing, as though it had just happened.

And I trembled, and my anger was a hot metal drum, banging out a horrible beat inside my head.

And then there was the window breaking and Jake McCormack invading the shop and taking our family book, and me making a decision then. The most important decision of my life.

There was to be no more dignified silence, no more exiting stage left, no more turning the other cheek.

I grabbed the car keys.

'Luca, where are you going?' Allie asked.

'I'm going after Jake.'

'No, please. Haven't I been trying all this time to tell you how dangerous he is? Don't you believe me?'

'Leave me alone, Allie, do you hear me? I've had enough.'

My mother tried too. 'Luca, *mi amore*,' she kept saying.

'I'm not your *amore*,' I told her. 'Stop saying that.'

Allie took my arm. 'Please don't do this. You've nothing to prove to anyone.'

She was wrong. I had plenty to prove. And there was only one way to do that.

CHAPTER 21

'I am Luca Spinelli,' I said to myself as I got in the car, 'and I am no longer going to let Jake McCormack prevail.'

I took the back lane that brings you round behind Clanfedden and loops around to the other side of the bridge. Catching him head-on. That was going to be my only chance.

As I drove, I made a promise to myself. History would not keep going around and around. Jake McCormack had bullied and tormented and terrorised the town of Clanfedden for long enough. Things were going to move forward, and I would learn from the past, and not be defined by it. And no one was going to threaten me or my mother like this. I'd had enough. Jake was not going to have power any more, and it was me, Luca Spinelli, who was going to make sure of it.

I thought about his woolly balaclava that covered his face on account of his terrible scars, and how he wore shades even when there was no sunshine. I thought about how he ran the town, how he was mean and quick to anger and how he controlled everyone.

I mightn't get another opportunity. There was no time to think it through. There is no need, when you know what has to be done.

Suddenly he was my only mission. I was chasing down Jake McCormack on behalf of anyone who'd ever been dominated or deceived or diminished or devastated.

Maybe this was going to be the end of me, but not going after him would also be the end of me, so you know, might as well make the righter choice, do the braver thing.

I'd driven round fast enough and over to the other side, and just as I'd planned, I'd managed to drive on to the bridge while he was barrelling over from the other direction.

I was aware of people running, I remember seeing their mouths move. Warning me.

'Stop!' they would be saying. 'You've got to back up, Luca! That is Jake McCormack!'

And I thought, Why would I do that? Now that I have him in my sights!

I drove forward in one direction and the truck drove forward towards me too, in the other. It kept coming towards me and everybody knows there is only room for one vehicle at a time on Clanfedden Bridge, and then we both picked up speed and now there were two of us, both driving at full speed towards one another.

It was only when we'd reached the very centre, where the dip is, that I screeched to a last-minute halt. And though I could not see his face because that was in darkness, Jake McCormack was staring down at me with all his power and all his might, and all around me I could see the people of Clanfedden starting to gather on either end of the bridge and they were yelling things, telling me to reverse, to back up, that I shouldn't be stupid.

But I grasped the steering wheel tighter than ever. I was sure that behind the balaclava and the shades, Jake McCormack was sneering at me.

I opened the car door then. I leapt out and walked right up to Jake's truck. I stood right in front, pounding on the grille at the front with my fist.

'Give me back my family's book!' I bellowed.

He shook his head just once. And still he sneered.

He mouthed something at me then. 'Get out of the way, boy.'

'You're in the way!' I screamed. 'You're the one who's in the way. You coward, sitting up there in your truck. *You* need to get out of the way!'

There was a gasp from the crowd.

I stared into the blank, black, sunglass-gaze of Jake McCormack.

'Luca, come on, enough. Get back in the car.' It was Allie. I saw others there too, then: and Conor and Poppy, and Rory Redmond and all our customers, begging me.

'You don't have a choice,' Allie said then.

'I do have a choice,' I said. 'Don't you see? I get to decide.'

Jake's truck screamed and revved.

'Decide what?' she asked.

I said nothing. I just locked my eyes with Jake's.

This was it.

They say some of the most important moments of your life happen in slow motion, and so it was. I see myself throwing my mother's car keys into the air and slowly, very slowly they tumble and I can hear their ringing, clear and true, like the sound of a small bell, and that little noise carries high above the growl of Jake's thundering truck – and all I can hear then is the chink and tinkle of the keys. And they seem to leave behind them a trail of beautiful light as they rise, bizarrely triumphant, and then as they fall.

And the splash beneath Clanfedden Bridge is like a fish breaking the surface of the flat water and there is a whirling eddy and the keys get sucked into the silky river. There are strands of riverweed black and swirling and I am proud to have done this disastrous thing and I am not afraid.

Some moments in life are their own victories, no matter what happens next.

If I'd lived to be a hundred, I'd still feel the power and the beauty and the wonder of it.

Jake's truck revved up even louder, belching out more black ghosts of smoke, until a great dark cloud hung over the bridge. There was another shudder then, and the truck moved forward, ineluctable.

I saw Allie, trying to get nearer but people held her back and I heard her shouting.

And the truth of what that girl meant to me became clearer than ever. I realised this, though it was too late.

She wanted to stop me, because she cared about me and she did not want me to do what I was going to do. And it didn't matter what Tom Cranfield had told her on the phone, and I didn't care that she had spoken to him.

I stood right in the middle, two fists in the air.

'Tu non puoi passere,' I shouted. *'Non devi prevalere.'*

You shall not pass. You shall not prevail.

I didn't really think it would make any difference, but it felt good to say those things.

Jake McCormack's truck stayed right in front of me and then lurched forward and that old rattle sounded like a swarm of insects and the two giant crusty ragged wheels rolled closer and I still I did not move.

And then all the breath was knocked out of me and everything hurt and being crushed by a six-foot tyre feels like I imagine drowning feels, and then there was Allie, kneeling beside me and telling me something I could not hear and me hoping I'd looked strong even if it was only for a moment, hoping she thought I was brave.

And I am on the ground, and I think I already know I am going to die, that the great nothing is coming. This is it. But before it comes there is one final comfort and it is Allie, and her voice, which still sounds like music, saying my name.

PART 5

DARK MORNING

ALLIE REDMOND

CHAPTER 22

There is a place in my head that will never go away now. A place where I will always see the brown velvet of late summer turning sour.

Luca went down, crumpling like paper under the wheels.

His body under Jake McCormack's truck. His face in the mud on the wrong side of Clanfedden Bridge. The blue lights and the sirens blaring, and him trying to speak and his face all smashed up. Jake's truck, unmoving, engine running. Everyone frozen.

'Call an ambulance,' someone screamed. 'Call the police,' someone else shouted, and just like that the scene sprang into life.

I ran to him; I knelt down. I can't remember who else was beside me.

'Oh, Luca,' I said. 'Why did you try to take him on?'

'Somebody had to.'

His voice was a thin little sound; his breath came in

gasps. I had to get very close to hear him and people were trying to pull me away.

'Allie,' he whispered. 'No matter what happens now, I'm never going to regret this. I'm always going to be glad I tried.'

'What do you mean, *no matter what happens now*?' I said. 'You're OK, Luca, you're grand. There's an ambulance coming.'

He closed his eyes.

'Somebody had to do it,' he whispered. 'I'm happy it was me.'

I should have said so many things to him then. I should have told him that I was lucky he was my friend, that he was good and kind and generous and brave. And that of course he could never have done anything wrong and I never should have imagined or suspected that he had.

And I should have said that I admired him for doing what none of us had the courage to do and stand up to Jake McCormack. But Luca's face had gone all white. And all I could do was say his name.

The paramedics came and, in the rush and panic, I got pulled and jostled out of the way. And Ariana went with him in the ambulance, and there were struggles and shouts, and I was on the outskirts of the crowd then, everyone looking strange and shimmery in the wobbly blue swivelling light. And the ambulance headed off with Luca and his mother inside.

Even in the wake of this violence and chaos I never expected, not in my darkest possible nightmare, to hear what I heard.

'He's dead,' somebody said. 'The boy is dead.'

And the whisper rippled around the crowd, that Luca Spinelli had just been killed on Clanfedden Bridge.

People had surrounded Jake McCormack's truck. Terry Morrison was banging on the side of it. Dogs were barking in the fields.

But Jake McCormack revved the engine again. His reverse lights were on. 'Get out of the way before he kills someone else!' came another voice in the crowd, and everyone did get out of the way as Jake's truck huge as it was, spun around and sped off.

Nobody had stopped him.

'What is wrong with this town?' I shouted. 'What is wrong with all of us?'

I wanted my mum. It was a childish unrealistic thing, but I spoke out loud to her.

'Mum, please help me,' I said, even though my mum was dead.

CHAPTER 23

You probably think it's the people you love most who you should keep your promises to, but this is not so. The most important promises you make are to the people you hate.

I will make Jake McCormack suffer for the things he has done. That was the promise I made.

The decision solidified inside my heart until there was nothing else left. I ran from the crowd and flung myself at my bike and I began to pedal after Jake's truck. There was a burning crackle in my head, like I was on fire. I followed the truck to the restaurant. I watched him as he wrote something on the door and when he got back into the truck, I went to read what it said: *'There are times when disagreeable decisions must be made.'* You bastard, I muttered to myself, cycling up Crookthorpe Hill after him, not taking my eyes off the red lights at the back of the truck, not stopping to take a breather, not even at the steepest part of that hill. I saw him turn in through the gaping gates. I heard them clang behind him.

I skidded to a halt, choking on the filthy fumes that spewed out from his blackened exhaust. My rage was so strong, there was almost the tinge of a thrill in it. My body trembled and sweated outside his fenced-in fortress. I was ready for anything. I dropped my bike to the ground, walked over, shook the gates.

The house was very big, a huge hulk of stone. There was a spiky high fence, and a camera at the gates.

There was a battered buzzer and I pressed it. Again and again and again. He would be inside by now and I knew he could hear it. Apart from my breathing, everything else was silent, the honeyed quiet of this place so different from the jumble of awful noises still echoing in my head.

I couldn't stop shivering and the blood would not stop pounding through my veins.

'It was not a disagreeable decision! It was murder! You monster. Let me in, Jake McCormack,' I screamed. 'Give me back what you have taken! Come out and stand in front of me! Face up to the wrong things you have done!'

I didn't care how long it was going to take.

I thought of how much Jake had taken from us and about the frightened people of Clanfedden whose lives he had wrecked. I thought about the Spinellis and the restaurant and the whole town meek under Jake's rule for so long.

But mainly, I thought about Luca. About his body going white and still in the dirt of the bridge.

'Come out, come out, Jake!' I shouted, over and over till my voice rasped. 'Come out, you coward.'

Ariana always said that bullies are all talk, full of menace and swagger but that they can be controlled, just as long as you stand up to him.

'There's something strange about a bully who never shows his face,' she said. 'All talk, no action. It's not real, Allie.'

But Ariana was wrong about that. Jake was dangerous and he was real. I thought then of the person who knew so much more than any of us – Veronica – and of what she had always said about Jake.

'He gets entertained by other people's distress. He enjoys seeing people in pain. It gives him a kind of a thrill. He takes what he wants, and he maims before he kills. If you cross him, he'll go after you. It's in his nature. He enjoys watching people scared and suffering.'

'Get out here, Jake McCormack, and face me,' I roared again.

And just then, there was a click and a beep and a swish and the gates swung open into the gravel driveway. I was hypnotised.

I left my bike by the open side of the gate, and I crunched my way to the door. I wasn't even scared.

I was ready.

I hammered on Jake's door. I wasn't expecting it to open, but slowly with a strange snarling sound, it did. At first I could not see much, then something moved in the blackness of that cold hallway, something glinted in the dark.

'You coward,' I whispered. 'Why don't you take off your mask?'

'Don't come any closer,' he said.

It wasn't a decision, what I did next. It was a crazy sort of impulse.

I grabbed the balaclava mask he always wore. I pulled it off him and I looked into his face.

And I saw. I understood.

And the whole world turned upside down, went strange and twisted and I knew the shock of it would never leave me. Nothing felt like it would again look bright or feel right.

'You won't get away with this.' My voice was small. Whatever courage I'd had, I lost it. I had to get away.

But the gates were shut. They had clamped behind me, and my bike had been mangled among the wrought-iron teeth.

I scrabbled away like a rat. I ran through the grounds. My palms slapped up against the spike-topped fence. I took a deep breath and I climbed.

There was a moment of balance at the top when I thought I'd done it. But then there was the nauseating topple, and a sharp pain in my thigh, worse than anything I'd ever felt.

That could have been it, and I could have stayed up there on Crookthorpe Hill, impaled on the top of that fence, like a horrible warning to anyone else who might have dared to try the same thing.

I heard the scraping of something heavy along the ground. I think I saw a ladder. I watched as though in a dream, because of how loud and huge the pain was, and clarity and logic was drowning and the darkness was swimming around me. I heard the creak of the ladder steps.

But all that happened was I got lifted off the spike I was stuck on. The lifting took a long time and I think I fainted maybe. I landed with an 'oof' from my lungs on to the concrete ground on the other side of the fence, and I didn't know if it was a nightmare or if it was real, or if it was just the wind in the trees.

'Help me, please,' I whispered.

'No, I will not help you,' came the answer, called over the fence. 'I am going to kill you.'

And I knew for sure this was true and something clear came to me, like the striking of a match in the dark. I knew that up there on the mountain, there was no help to be got, and I was only going to be able to rely on myself. This was my last chance, and I didn't have much time.

'Think smart,' I told myself.

I struggled to my hands and knees and I stood. And then I started to limp away.

The wind shrieked, whipping at the creaking trees and whistling through cracks in the thick Clanfedden rock. The night was an unnatural inky black and I struggled through the scraggy tangle of rusted fences. There was malice in the bushes, the scratching brambles, the stabbing thorns. I gritted my teeth against the pain. My leggings were wet with blood, all the way down to my ankle.

I stumbled over some jagged rock and I fell. I lay there gasping.

And then I heard it.

I heard the roar of the truck, its jerks and squeaks getting closer. I fumbled for my phone, turned it on. A signal appeared. I had signal. The miracle of it was like a light in the dark.

I pressed a button. Dad.

He answered right away, as though the phone had barely rung.

'Oh, Allie, peanut, thank goodness!' was all he said, and it was a long time since he'd called me that, and he was not angry, and his voice was the sound of home. 'Where are you, Allie? Tell me. Wherever you are, I'll come.'

There were so many things I wanted to say but there was no time.

'Dad, listen to me. I've been up to Crookthorpe. I wanted to see Jake McCormack. And oh, Dad, I've something to tell you, though I can hardly believe it myself, and I need you to please come. Please help me.'

'Allie, just tell me where you are.'

I suppose I should have expected what happened next.

My phone died.

'Dad,' I whisper. 'Dad, I'm so sorry.'

CHAPTER 24

I'll never know how I managed it.

But I did. Keeping my head down so that the beam from the truck's headlights couldn't find me, listening the whole time for its rattle, I did it. I got myself off the mountain and into town.

I passed the station and the stables, and I crossed Main Street, over the bridge, trying not to think about what happened there.

There is no silence like small-town-night-time quiet. I let myself breathe. I knew I was very close to Dad.

I heard gentle music playing then, though there was none. I felt warm suddenly as I got to the door of my house and pressed my face against it.

I cried then. Because the light was on and I had come so far, and it was the lifting of the burden and the easing of the fear that had been hounding me.

But when I hammered on the door, Dad didn't answer.

Strings of silence weaved around me, cold and dark and indifferent. And there was nothing else, except the injured echoes of my own weakening voice.

And my pain grew worse and different – twisting inside me as if there is a special kind of poisonous agony reserved for the desperate and the abandoned. The impossible journey I'd made seemed blurred and cloudy. I slumped down to the ground. The pain. It was was like some creature was clinging to my leg, bloated but hungry, threatening to gobble me up completely.

I don't know how long I lay there, but I do know that human despair has a sound. I hope you've never heard it and I hope you never will. It's a noise beyond screaming: the low growl of the animal that's in us all.

There was a click and a rustle and, through the fog, I saw a shape coming towards me. This was it. I had been pursued and I had been found and now I was going to be killed.

But it was Dad. He was out of breath. There were tears on his face. He knelt down beside me.

'Allie, Jesus, bloody hell, Allie, I've been looking for you everywhere. Thank goodness, oh thank God.' He saw my leg then and he gasped and fumbled for his own phone, talking to me all the time:

'Oh, Allie sweetheart, it's all right, I'm here,' and I could see that he had his determined face on now, his fixing face, the expression he used to have when Mum was alive and when he thought anything was possible. He talked on the phone and then hung up.

'It's all right, it's OK,' said Dad. 'I'm putting you in the car. An ambulance is on is way to us. We'll meet them halfway. We have to get you to hospital fast.'

Dad lifted me up and carried me to the car and laid me down on the back seat and he spoke in whispers, looking at my leg.

I took his hand. I held it firm.

'Dad, listen,' I said. 'There's something I need to tell you. I'm going to be killed, just like Luca was.'

And Dad said, 'No, Allie, I promise that's not going to happen. There'll be no more damage done in this town, my darling love, I'm not going to let it.'

Part of me wanted to trust him but I couldn't because he didn't know.

'Dad, Dad. Listen to me. You have to listen. Nothing is the way we thought it was. I've seen Jake McCormack. I know who Jake McCormack is.'

And before I could explain any further, two beams of yellowing light fell across our faces. I was the only one who knew what this meant.

Dad stood in front of me looking like he was getting ready for anything, but I knew. I knew he wasn't ready for this.

The handbrake creaked and the door cracked open and somebody got out of Jake's truck, and slowly that somebody began to walk towards us too.

They spoke.

'Rory, Allie, thank God. Don't be frightened. It's only me! I've come to help.'

I screamed. I screamed with all I had. 'Dad, listen to me, close the door! For God's sake, you mustn't let her in.'

'Allie,' Dad said. 'It's OK. It's just Veronica.'

But I knew. I'd seen the truth up at Crookthorpe and it had followed me down into the town. When I'd pulled Jake's balaclava off him in the doorway of his house, it was not the scarred face of Jake that was underneath.

It was the face of Veronica Grassbloom.

PART 6

THE TRUTH

VERONICA GRASSBLOOM

CHAPTER 25

I am Veronica Grassbloom and I am also Jake McCormack. It would of course come as a surprise to the people of Clanfedden. They must never know.

I deserved some recognition and respect around here, and inventing Jake McCormack turned out to be my only way of getting it. I wanted to make something of myself. And to do that I needed to be strong and fierce and powerful. Nobody took Veronica Grassbloom seriously. If I was going to be powerful, then I was going to have to invent someone else.

That's why I created him and I became him, speaking in a voice I had devised carefully, a voice that I imagined a man like Jake McCormack would have.

I don't quite know what gave me the idea, but when I had it, I was delighted by its genius. Maybe it was the thousands of stories I'd read, rich and old, a lifetime's inspiration. Jake came to me years ago, a genie taking shape from the fumes of my imagination.

Clanfedden had plenty of good guys, I figured. What we'd needed was a proper baddie. Someone to fear. Someone to blame.

I sipped from the occasional small glass of sherry up at the Clanfedden Inn, and I helped to spread the story around. Friends of friends who had suffered at the hands of Jake McCormack. How he got those scars. Why he always covered his face.

I had been convincing about the menace that was Jake McCormack. To tell the truth, it was exciting. Being him.

The people of Clanfedden loved Veronica Grassbloom, who went to bed in the basement of the library, shuffling down the stone staircase with her cocoa and her hot water bottle.

They did not know that then I snuck up the hill to Crookthorpe and hid my little car around the back, where the giant Crookthorpe House lay empty. I had bought it quietly, years ago. It seemed like the sort of place that Jake McCormack would live.

I rigged up the electric gates myself. I bought the truck, suitably dirty and battered. It was exactly the kind of vehicle that the likes of Jake McCormack would drive. I hired Brian to be my eyes and ears and run the betting shop, knowing that he wouldn't see further than his own nose.

Jake's business grew fast. He knew how to find out about people's weaknesses, knew how to offer them what they needed – and then exact a terrible price.

The money rolled in. Soon Clanfedden became less and less the town it had been and more and more a hushed place. A place ruled by one man.

Jake had to go out sometimes, of course. Had to survey his empire. Late some nights I would cover myself with a careful disguise, driving the truck around the town, hiding my face so no one knew it was just their old librarian. Menacing them just by sitting there, watching.

I sometimes laughed behind my mask. People stopped what they were doing, staring as I passed, but they never once realised who it really was.

Until she came back.

Ariana. She had already wrecked my life once.

Rachel was *my* best friend. When we were thirteen, we made a pact that nothing would ever come between us.

But less than a year after that promise, Ariana arrived and that was the summer everything changed. I did my best to hold on to her. I did my best to get her back.

But summer holiday after summer holiday Ariana came,

her parents having fallen in love with the place as much as she had, and summer after summer they left me out of things.

It was Ariana who threw a street party for Rachel's birthday the last summer she came, and she put lights up around the tennis court fencing. They condescended to invite me, but by then I would not humiliate myself – I could no longer be witness to their in-jokes and their shared delights, and the secrets they had that no one else knew.

That was the night Ariana announced she was going to chef school and that she wouldn't be back for a while. I was delighted when I heard this news. I was going to get Rachel back at last. I thought that it would just be us again, now that Ariana wouldn't keep waltzing in every June, acting like she was better than everyone else, acting like she deserved to be Rachel's best friend.

I couldn't wait for the end of that summer. We'd have parties of our own after Ariana was gone, I thought.

But that didn't happen. Rachel fell in love with Rory. Ariana had been the one who brought them together by telling Rory that Rachel really liked him, by telling Rachel that Rory felt the same. Nobody had any interest in me any more. It was as if I was invisible. None of this would have happened if Ariana had never come. She was the one who took everything away from me.

Well, I am strong now, and can play that kind of game too, I thought to myself.

I did everything right. I was kindly, sympathetic Veronica. Friend of the family.

I waited.

Like most myths, Jake got larger. Each time the story of him was passed on, his power became more pronounced, richer with detail. I never once remember describing him to anyone, but soon the town had it that his face was horribly scarred and terrifying to see.

Jake McCormack was also making a world of difference in Clanfedden. Everyone was meek now, minding their manners. All they had to do was get the slightest hint that Jake McCormack didn't approve of something, and that something would immediately stop.

Meanwhile good old Veronica kept her head down. The library job was perfect, because of the post office. I liked sorting the bundles of letters every week. I knew Ariana's handwriting – looping, extravagant, ridiculous – and saw her letters for Rachel. Every week. For years.

Of course I opened them up and I read them – just to check if she ever mentioned me, which she never did. Apart from asking Rachel about herself, she mostly wrote a load of narcissistic garbage about chef school and wanting those food stars, and all the things she was learning and all the men she was seeing. And there was a card when her boy was born. Anyway, I'd rip them up into thousands of tiny pieces and throw them away. There was satisfaction in that, I suppose. Rachel thought she had forgotten her.

Eventually the letters stopped coming completely and it made me feel glad that I'd played my part in terminating their friendship, just as Ariana had terminated mine. People might say I acted out of jealousy, but it's not true. It was *justice* I was after.

Your friends can't turn their backs on you without there being some kind of retribution. It doesn't matter how long ago it happened. And there was no point in anyone telling me, 'Oh, Veronica, it's all such a long time ago!' What does time have to do with anything? And it might seem sensible to suggest that you should put things of the past behind you, but you can't put something behind you when it's on your doorstep, when day after day, year after year you see other people happy at your expense, while you're watching your own lonely years slide off the edge of a cliff.

I did a lot of good things for Clanfedden that nobody knew about. A library does not stock itself. No one even bothered to ask how I'd managed to double the collection there. That was a gift. A gift from me to the soul of this town. I used the money from the betting shop to good effect. It wasn't all for me.

People need the library. Take Allie Redmond for example. She had always been the best reader in the town. I could hardly keep her in books. She read everything I lent her, and she would keep coming back, sometimes the same day, looking for more.

That's how I knew something was up, that spring. She hadn't checked out a book for more than three months. I suppose that had been the first sign for me. I wondered what could be wrong. No one can spot the heartache of a reader quicker than a librarian can.

She came to the library eventually, one day. And well, that was the day I found out how sick Rachel was and I suppose my hard heart began to thaw a little. Pitiful sobs from behind the shelves, Allie's small face stained and shiny with tears.

Bad times had come to the Redmond family. Rachel's terrible sickness was going to kill her in the end, and Allie, so young and so knotted up in this anguish and worrying about money and about medicine. Such things are generally of no interest to children, since most children are not embroiled in sadness and not facing great loss on the near horizon. I would help her get the money. Of course I would. Who wouldn't?

And besides, it was going to be my opportunity to re-establish my friendship, with Rory and now with Allie. I imagined myself at the centre of that family. I was going to be able to help, and after that there was nothing they wouldn't do for me. It could be like the old days.

The online medicine might have worked. I warned Allie of the danger of borrowing money from Jake McCormack.

It had to be him, of course; no one else had that sort of money.

But the medicine did not work, and Rachel died.

I didn't appreciate it when Rory came to the library and humiliated me by scolding me for my act of charity. How dare I help to encourage his daughter to get into debt, and under such false pretences! But I took it. I even apologised and cried, and he felt sorry for me then and it was easy to be humble, because I already knew how I was going to restore the balance.

Now there was money to be owed. And that was that. Business is business.

I tormented them for weeks about the debt. I cannot say it didn't give me pleasure.

I remember Allie's frightened face at the library when she told me that Jake McCormack had rung seventeen times in one day, how scared she and Rory were.

'Oh, you poor things,' I'd said. 'The audacity and nastiness of that man.'

It was a genius stroke, I thought, cancelling the debt.

It would be a small price to pay, I thought, for their gratitude and their love. And it was a delicious kind of deceit.

And, for a while, things were lovely again. I saw them all the time. It was like having a family, the family I should have had. And I knew Rory thought so too.

But then, when I tried to take it further, he pulled away

from me, and, oh goodness, how I detest men who don't know what they want.

I didn't realise that Rory Redmond and his cronies had got organised. They had evidence of intimidation. Emails, recorded phone calls and whatnot. The official complaint came through the town council and the leasing company agreed to co-operate. And that was how the leasing company got wind of the so-called 'damaging practices' being conducted by me, undermining Clanfedden's good name, apparently, and injuring the reputation of this town.

It was Rory's fault that my lease was cancelled. The Redmonds brought down my business with their meddling and whining.

'Just set up somewhere else,' Brian Freeman had suggested at first. As if Jake McCormack lies down and goes away.

I couldn't believe it when she came back, when she bought my shop. Talk about rubbing it in my face. That witch Ariana came back to wreck everything again.

I tried to act as if I was glad she was back in town. I watched her business grow and blossom. Watched the whole of Clanfedden go to Spinellis' to stuff their greedy faces.

They forgot all about the library, the book fair. I was

surplus to requirements again. A curse on you, Ariana, for upstaging me like you have always done. She had taken Rachel away from me and she had taken Rory, slowly, over those summers long ago, turning them away from me. And now she was taking Allie, hiring her to work in that place. Everything I had ever wanted, stolen from under my nose.

Veronica Grassbloom could never be angry. Veronica Grassbloom was too decent and good and kind a person to behave like that. It was up to Jake McCormack to act.

Allie waited outside the gates at Crookthorpe for a long time. How I wished I could have granted mercy. But I was no longer Veronica. I was Jake.

Last night, when it became clear that she wasn't going to go away, I opened the gates. In the darkened hallway I knew what would have to be done. I knew it even before she tried to escape. And I still know it now. I have killed a boy on Clanfedden Bridge. And now that it is morning, I must find and kill the girl too. As I say, she won't have got far, and I must find her before the rest of the world discovers my secret.

PART 7

THE RAGE

CHAPTER 26
ALLIE

'Veronica,' my dad says slowly. 'Just as a matter of interest, what are you doing with Jake McCormack's truck?'

'That's a rather complicated story,' she replies, plunging her hands deep into the pockets of her dark, oversized jacket.

Veronica was supposed to have been my second mother. Of all the people I could trust, she was supposed to have been the most trustworthy.

And now she is watching us and there is a blackness round her eyes and her hair is wild and her clothes are ripped.

'I know who you are! I understand everything now!' I shout at her.

'Well,' she says, and her voice is different now, it's his voice, a slow, frightening drawl. 'Well now. Perhaps that's the problem. Perhaps that's exactly why you can't be allowed to continue. You and your stupid father here.'

From her black jacket, Veronica pulls a knife. Big and gleaming and hatchet-like, and she is mad, properly mad, and I'm thinking, *this is it.*

Veronica Grassbloom spits out a mountain of rage. Old dwelled-upon grudges from a far distant childhood.

'We were friends, weren't we?' she says. 'Me and you and Rachel. But then Ariana came to town, didn't she? Rachel was *mine*. We'd planned to have all manner of adventures together. But guess who she had those adventures with in the end? She had them with Ariana Spinelli. That woman robbed me of the thousands of happy days I should have spent with my friend. I was dismissed. I have been diminished.'

The massive knife flashes and glints. 'Well, you can't dismiss or diminish me now, can you?'

Her laughter is a crazy ragged thing and there is something vicious deep inside it.

'It's OK, Vonnie,' my dad says, moving between me and her. 'It's OK.'

She moves fast, and I'm watching from inside the car, and now she's holding the knife to my dad's neck. 'Don't move,' she says, spittle bubbling through her teeth.

'I won't, Vonnie,' Dad says, and he's trying to glance back at me all the time as the tip of the knife draws a line on his skin. 'I won't tell anyone. It can be our secret.'

'Wait now, let me see. I'm not sure I can really trust you. I mean, I haven't been able to trust you in the past, now have I? No; I think there's only one thing to be done.' She smiles. 'Yes, my dears, I'm afraid I'm going to have to kill you both! Sorry it has come to this, but as I say, I don't see that there is any other option.'

She draws her hand back and everything seems to slow down, and the edges of the knife wobble like liquid as it lunges towards my dad.

'Allie, call Ariana!' he shouts at me, and I know what he means, and I see Veronica's fury rising up and I see my dad rising up to meet it.

They lunge at each other. I cannot see the knife now even though I know it's still there. All I can see is my dad and Veronica locked in a frightening wrestle of love and of hate.

'You will not hurt my girl,' he shouts. But she is in a frenzy now and she gets him to the ground, grabbing both his wrists, kneeling on his legs. She looks towards me and cackles and it is a horrible noise.

A jolt shudders through me. For just a second, my pain seems to disappear, and I feel the rage inside my own damaged body, and this time the rage is not a bad thing. This time the rage is going to save us.

'You will not hurt my dad!' I shout and I haul myself out of the car and still I do not feel the pain I should be feeling as I kick her off balance and the knife skitters and slides across the path.

'Quick,' Dad says, picking me up and more or less throwing me back in the car. He dashes to the front seat, slams the door shut, starts the engine before she's even struggled to her feet. I can hear her screams fading as we speed away:

'I will not be punished!' she screams. 'I will not!'

'It's going to be OK, Allie,' says Dad, but I don't know if he is right and I am dizzy and I slip into stillness.

'Stay with me, Allie,' Dad says and I can hear the howl of a siren.

I dream that my mother's hand is on my forehead, gently brushing my hair, but even in the dream I know she hasn't come back to me, that I am just reaching for her and longing for her and needing her, and that the memory of her is going to have to do.

When I open my eyes, I'm being transferred to an ambulance and people are telling me I am great and Dad is saying how proud he is of me.

'Why are you proud of me?' I whisper.

'Because you're brave,' he says. 'You chased after a murderer on your own. I mean, never do it again or anything, but Allie, you're so courageous for wanting to make things right. And you got all the way back down to Clanfedden from high up on Crookthorpe Hill, on your own, after everything that's happened, in this condition. What voices did you need to silence? What promises did you have to make to yourself?'

'I was wrong about everything,' I said. 'I thought Veronica

was kind and I thought she cared about me, but she's held this town to ransom all these years, and now look at the horrible, dreadful things she has done, and I was supposed to do something about it at last, but I ran away, from the trouble and the danger. That's what I did in the end. I ran away. I didn't fix anything.'

'Running away is sometimes the bravest thing of all, Allie. It takes great and awesome wisdom.'

'But Luca is dead,' I say.

'Don't say that, love,' he replies, holding my hand tight. 'How can you be sure?'

'Everyone was saying it, on the bridge.'

'Just because everyone says something doesn't mean it's true.'

But I know it is.

Veronica is dead too, in a way. I remember how she had calmed my soul, and how important she said imagination was and how we must keep it alive no matter what. She opened a world of books to me. And I will grieve for her, the person I thought she was.

'She was supposed to have been my safety! She was supposed to have been my refuge!' I sob.

And Dad says, 'Allie, you don't need her any more because you have me now. I'll be your safety, my darling, and I'll be your refuge. I'm sorry I haven't been those things for the last few years, but I will be from now on.'

And everything is blurred, and thoughts are splashing

in my head and even though it's great to hear my dad say these things, still I can't stop being afraid.

The siren sounds louder and faster. Everything feels dark and complicated and close-up.

I cry for the pain I am in and for the frightened girl I still am, and I cry for my mum and for the Veronica I have lost and for the Jake she has become and for Luca's life and for Ariana who believed everything was going to be all right.

Between sleeping and waking I remember my dad telling me Veronica has been arrested, that everyone on the bridge turned her in. She's in custody.

They are ready for us at the hospital. There is a blur of colour when they bring me in, and then the tinkle and clash of hospital noises.

There is a lot of hurried talk then between my dad and the doctors and nurses and medics. Their voices are low and solemn and then I see a light above me like the beam of a truck, but I know it's an operating room and there are three people bent over me, wearing masks, and then I don't know anything else.

When I open my eyes again, there is my dad still, like he's always going to be beside me. My leg is now bandaged. The pain is much better.

Dad puts his hand on my forehead and brushes my hair out of my face, and then he speaks low and quiet. 'Allie, how are you feeling?'

'OK,' I say.

We sit there for a while and he tells me about the operation and how my leg is going to be perfectly fine, it isn't as bad as they thought. It is going to be a while before I'll be able to walk again, and after that I am going to have to do exercises to get it strong.

I'm only half listening, and Dad knows this.

'Would you like to see Luca?' he asks, at last.

I need to see him. I know that, but I am dreading it.

I'm going to have to be stronger than ever, but I am weak now and very sad. This is going to be the biggest grown-up moment in my life so far. I am going to have to look at what I cannot bear to see, which is, something we all must do sometimes.

It takes them a while to move me into a wheelchair. My dad keeps wincing even though it's me who has the injured leg. 'That's it, love, good woman,' says a nurse who arranges a blanket over my knees like I'm a very old person. Dad is the one who pushes me out of the ward and along the hospital corridor right down to the end and into the lift and up to another floor with the kind nurse leading the way all chatty. How can she be so happy, I wonder when we're on our way to see Luca. The lights above blare down, and the nurse's happy voice melds with the clang of metal, the swivel of wheels, the whoosh of curtains, the padding sounds of fast walking feet in soft shoes. We come to a sign that says 'special unit'. My dad turns the wheelchair around, the nurse holds the door open and whispers 'I'll leave you to it,' winking at me, and in we go to that darkened, hushed room, with the doors closing gently behind us.

Ariana's sitting beside his bed. Her hair seems wilder than ever and her face is puffy and red like she's been crying all night. Dad wheels me over, and puts his hand for a moment on Ariana's shoulder.

'Ariana,' I say, but she puts a finger to her lips and says only, 'Your father and I will leave you with him for a little while. Come, Rory,' she beckons. He nods. 'We'll see you shortly, Allie. We're just outside if you need us.'

There he is, his poor broken body wrapped up in plaster and bandages and his lovely face, so bruised, and his closed eyes swollen.

'Luca,' I say softly. 'Oh, Luca.'

I reach out to touch his lifeless hand.

But his hand is warm. The machines beside him are beeping – and there in the hush, I realise that they've always been beeping.

Luca Spinelli opens his eyes and turns his head towards me.

A spark flies from the spot where our hands are touching, or maybe it is the sun, which has risen and is blazing now in through the frosted window, making everything suddenly bright, suddenly clear.

He smiles a tired smile.

'You're not dead,' I say, very quietly.

'*Brava!*' His voice is all sand and glue. 'Glad you noticed.'

'Nurse, Nurse!' I yell.

'What are you shouting for?'

'We have to get your mum and the nurses and the doctors! We have to tell them!'

'Everyone knows. This is a hospital,' he laughs. 'They're quite good at spotting the difference between the alive patients and the dead ones.'

'Oh, Luca. Luca, you're OK.'

He isn't really OK. He looks like a mummy. But he is alive, and because of this, a million things are again possible.

'It only hurts if I talk too loud. Are you OK yourself?'

'Yes, I am,' I say. 'I mean, I will be.'

And we are both silent and I am full of complicated feelings.

'There are so many things I have to tell you, Luca,' I say at last.

I explain everything to him then, how Veronica is Jake. How I had trusted her all these years.

I tell him about my shame, about the money I'd borrowed and how much trouble it had brought, about all the confusion.

'I let her get my family in her clutches. I didn't see. I didn't realise. I was a total fool.'

'Allie, you were not a fool. You were trying to save your mum. That's not foolish. That's brave.'

'Yeah right. A strange kind of brave.'

'All bravery is strange,' he says then.

'If it wasn't for me, Dad wouldn't have done the petition to get Jake out, and the betting shop wouldn't have been sold and you and your mum wouldn't have come and you'd have been safe – and when you think about it, this is all my fault too. If it wasn't for me none of this would have happened.'

'Allie, me and my mother coming here is the best thing I could have possibly ever imagined. I'll never regret it,'

'How can you even say that?' I say, looking at the stains of bruises, purple and yellow on his face.

'I got to meet you, didn't I? And Spinellis' is here now and there's no taking that away. And the town is saved from the myth of Jake McCormack, thanks to you.'

'Yeah, OK, true. And you're going to be OK.'

'Don't speak too soon. I could still die,' he says cheerfully.

'Nope,' I reply. 'It's not an option. You dying is not really on the cards. You're too important. Clanfedden would grind to a halt without you now. You've got to stay alive.'

'OK then,' Luca laughs, 'I'll do my best.'

And he keeps on chuckling, with his body all covered in plaster.

*

We spend a week in the hospital together, a time I will never forget. We talk about everything – including what happened back at Luca's old school.

He tells me the whole story and I feel angry for him.

'My bruised face was nothing,' he says. 'I'd got over that in a few days. And my fear was already gone. But Allie, the video, there was a video of the whole bloody thing and because of that I thought it would be with me for ever.

'I thought it was going to follow me around for the rest of my life. It was never going to leave me alone. There was a kind of deadness inside me. I can't explain it better than that. And then when I realised there was a bully here too . . . Well, I said, this time, this time the bad guy's not going to prevail.'

I remember then that day in the library, hunting for information about the new boy in town, and how every single click on the name *Luca Spinelli* had led to nothing but a dead end.

ERROR 404
The server cannot find what was requested
Image no longer available
This video has been removed
You do not have permission to view this link

There was a reason we couldn't find anything about Luca online.

Ariana and one of Luca's old teachers had found out that a video existed and was doing the rounds online. It's possible to get online material taken out of the public domain. You have to email a lot of people, including the owner of Google and the CEO of YouTube and make a strong case that the video infringes your human rights, but Ariana and the teacher had been determined and in the end they did it. I'm glad they took it down, but I want Luca to know it wouldn't have mattered if they'd left it up.

'Stupid videos of people are everywhere,' I tell him. 'Nobody cares. There isn't a video in the world that could change Clanfedden's mind about you. Everyone in this town thinks so highly of you.'

'Good to know,' he says chirpily. 'But more important than that, what do *you* think of me?'

'I think highly of you too,' I say, knowing this doesn't even come close.

'As a matter of fact, I think you're pretty much the best thing ever.'

PART 8

THE FINISH

CHAPTER 27

There was a lot of confusion on the day I was supposed to have died.

Rumours travel around this town very easily, regardless of whether they are right or wrong.

I'm glad to say the death rumours were not true. They only lasted a few minutes, but by then Allie had gone after Jake, to avenge my having died, which as I say, thankfully I actually had not done.

Everyone in the hospital was very kind. After the truck rolled over me, I'd been unconscious for over half an hour. When I woke up, I had to translate almost everything my mother said for the medical team because she'd reverted completely to Italian.

I slept and woke and slept and woke and eventually Allie was there.

We talked and talked, like we couldn't stop.

'None of this would have happened if it hadn't been for

me borrowing money from a phantom man who was really Veronica all along.'

Allie cried then, and my mother hugged her for a long time and said, 'There, there, *mi amora*, all is well.'

And she explained to Allie that she didn't care about anything, not the car, not the book. 'We'll get that recipe book back,' I insisted, remembering the last time I'd seen it was in Jake McCormack's hands.

'Ah well, now, as long as you two are all right, this is all that matters to me. Belongings are nice, and yes some of them are precious, indeed they are. But it does not do to load too much mystical power into things; objects are not that important, no matter how much we think they represent.'

'But all the recipes! For the restaurant! How could Veronica have taken them away from us too?'

'Don't you remember, my dear. We know those recipes off by heart.

'Here is where my recipes are,' she said, thumping her chest.

Not long after that, Poppy and Conor arrived too, and they had brought books and board games. It was kind of great to be able to tell them the whole story. They couldn't believe it either. We were going to be talking about it for a long, long time. They stayed for ages until the head nurse came in and told us to keep it down, that we weren't the only patients in this hospital.

*

Before he left, Conor lent me his charger. When I switched on my phone, of course, there were the string of texts. I opened one and then a few more. They all said the same thing. How he was very sorry for what had happened. How he'd been trying to get in touch. His latest one said he just heard I'd been a hero in Clanfedden last night. And then his number started flashing and of course it was Tom Cranfield and for some reason, still injured and wrecked, it was the moment when I finally felt able to answer him.

'Hey, Tom,' I croaked.

'Hey, Luca. Wow, man. Thanks for answering. You've been hard to get.'

'Yeah, I know. What can I do for you?'

'Are you still in hospital? Are you OK? I can't believe you tried to stand up to a madman in a monster truck!'

'I'm fine. How did you hear about that?'

Conor had told his cousin, who had told his mates, who told Tom.

'Well done to you, man.'

'Thanks,' I said again.

'Hey, Luca, look, the thing is, I've been feeling really bad about everything that happened and the truth is I can't stop thinking about it. I felt bad already, but when I'd heard that you left Dublin because of me, that's when I started feeling really lousy. I've been trying to get a hold of you ever since.'

'How do you know it was because of you?'

'Because of what I did. Because of how horrible I was.'

'Right, OK,' I said. 'Well, don't beat yourself up. A lot of stuff has happened since then. You were horrible all right and you did a dreadful thing, but, like, I'm not obsessing about it or anything. Not any more.'

There was a kind of pause then.

'I thought maybe there might be some way of making it up to you,' he said.

'No, Tom, no there isn't,' I said, and it felt good to tell him the truth, simple and clear like that.

'OK, but, well, look, I don't want there to be any hard feelings between us. I mean, at least let me ask you one of your questions,' he said then.

'What do you mean?'

'You know, like who would win in a fight between Godzilla and King Kong or between Superman and Batman, or between an electric eel or a poison jellyfish or something.'

'Tom,' I said. 'To be honest, I'm not really interested in those kinds of things any more.'

'Oh right,' he said, sounding a little disappointed. 'Anyway, look mate. I'm really sorry.'

'It's OK,' I said. I meant it.

'Great! I'm so glad. Thanks, Luca. Really, that means a lot to me. Maybe I could come visit. Maybe we could hang out.'

'Leave that with me for a while,' I said, shaking my head,

because in reality there was no way in hell Tom Cranfield and I were going to hang out ever again.

Lots of things in Clanfedden were still going to happen. Terry Morrison was going to fish the keys of my mother's car out of Clanfedden river and Brian Freeman was going to repair it, and Spinellis' glass front was going to get fixed and the restaurant was going to become even more famous, and because of it, Clanfedden was going to become one of the top ten towns to visit in Ireland.

And the cloud of fear that had hovered over this town was going to lift. Brian Freeman was going to take over the library because Veronica Grassbloom was going to go to jail for all the terrible things she had done, and the story of what had happened was going to spread far beyond Clanfedden and everyone who heard it was going to be amazed.

And Veronica was going to send us a parcel that had Jake McCormack's hat in it, and Jake McCormack's shades and Jake McCormack's jacket, and the Spinelli family recipe book. And a lot of other things were going to happen too. But that was the future, and it's not a good idea to dwell too much on things that haven't yet happened.

But right now, here in the hospital, the only thing I want to do is keep looking at Allie and her face is a beautiful thing even when her forehead is crumpled with worry.

'Honestly, Allie, I'm OK,' I tell her, for the hundredth time.

'But what about your poor body?' she says, and for a moment I think she might be about to cry.

'Listen, Allie, seriously, no harm done,' I say, and instead of crying, we begin to laugh at what a ridiculous thing that is to have said, what with Allie being in a wheelchair and her face stained with tears and me bandaged up on the bed barely able to move.

And the laughter seems give life back to us and we keep on laughing, louder and louder, like we are singing some brilliant crazy song. Our laughter fills the air and it spills out into the corridor and a great bubble of sunshine bursts in.

It is as if this sound might lift the whole hospital off its foundations and somehow we might float away, through the Limerick skies and northwards to Clanfedden, beyond the school and the garage and the bridge and the library. Above the twinkling playground, and the green tennis courts, and Spinellis' restaurant will shine back up at us.

And the sun is going to turn the Clanfedden River blue and the light in the trees will glow radiant, and a breeze will whisper soft through the leaves and branches. And our pain will not kill us. And things are going to be all right. And we can start again.

THE END

ACKNOWLEDGEMENTS

The heartiest of thanks to Ben Moore and Melanie Sheridan, my two very cherished early readers. To Helen Thomas who has made this book with me, and to Jo Unwin for being so brilliant and so lovely.

I'm hugely grateful also to Louise O'Neill, Eoin Devereux, Kit de Waal, Noel and Sadb Harrington, Bob and Adele Whelan, Dan Mooney, Sheila Killian, Jennifer O'Dea, Caroline O'Dea, Julie Hamilton, Fionnuala Price, Sarah MacCurtain, Geri Maye and Siobhan Tierney.

A particular note of gratitude to Joe O'Dea without whose gracious support this story would have taken a great deal longer to write, and to my very own ray of creative sunshine, Gráinne O'Brien.

To my beloved UL colleagues, Joseph O'Connor, Donal Ryan, Kerry Neville and Martin Dyar and to all the students on the MA in creative writing, past and present.

To Eoghan, Stef and Gabbie, my fabulous children; to Elizabeth Moore, my wonderful mum; to Zoey, Alma and Aoife, my newest nieces; and to Ger, my constant star.

More from

SARAH MOORE FITZGERALD

'The ghosts in your life don't ever really go away.
Every so often they will whisper to you ...
Don't worry about it too much.'

ISBN: 9781444007091

When Cosmo keeps his promise to his granddad to go to Blackbrick, he finds himself in the forgotten corner of a distant past, one that his granddad has, strangely, never really talked about. Here friendships come to life, there are new beginnings, a lifetime of memories and everything is still possible ...

More from

SARAH MOORE FITZGERALD

ISBN: 9781444011159

Oscar Dunleavy is missing, presumed dead.

His bike was found at sea, beyond the pier, and everyone in town has accepted this as a teenage tragedy.

Except for his best friend, Meg.

Oscar's kind, always cheerful, and makes the world's best apple tarts.

Meg knows he isn't dead ...

... and she's going to prove it.

More from

SARAH MOORE FITZGERALD

Some people step through a wardrobe to find adventure, but Minty follows the twisty-turny trees into Nettlebog. There she finds Ned Buckley – the moody, mysterious boy who never talks at school.

As Minty's world disintegrates around her she searches for refuge in Nettlebog, and she discovers more about Ned: he's able to ride wild horses. And he knows things about the human race that will save her.

Or at least there's a very good chance ...

More from

SARAH MOORE FITZGERALD

Grace knows the difference between what's real and the strange ideas that float around in her little sister's mind.

Their parents died – that's real. A secret hotel on the cliff-top where their parents are waiting – definitely NOT real.

When grief strikes again, Grace is determined not to let her sister's outlandish imagination spiral out of control. But the line between truth and fantasy is more complicated than it seems ...